"You Don't Have To Pay Me Back,"

Boone insisted.

That voice. So low and husky. So slow and sexy. Every time Boone said something, it sent a ripple of delight buzzing through Lucy's libido.

She ignored him and said, "Here's what I'm going to do—"

"Lucy…like I keep telling you, it's not necessary to pay me back for anything. Okay?"

Lucy hurried on. "Here's the deal. I'm giving you myself for one month."

When he seemed not to understand, Lucy tried again. "I'm yours to do your bidding, at your beck and call, for four weeks."

He still seemed mystified.

Finally, in an effort to make it as clear as possible, Lucy told him, "For the next thirty days, Boone Cagney, I'll do whatever you tell me to do. Because for the next thirty days, I'm going to be your slave."

THE FAMILY McCORMICK: Three separated siblings find each other—and love along the way!

Dear Reader;

A sexy fire fighter, a crazy cat and a dynamite heroine—that's what you'll find in *Lucy and the Loner,* Elizabeth Bevarly's wonderful MAN OF THE MONTH. It's the next in her installment of THE FAMILY McCORMICK series, and it's also a MAN OF THE MONTH book you'll never forget—warm, humorous and very sexy!

A story from Lass Small is always a delight, and *Chancy's Cowboy* is Lass at her most marvelous. Don't miss out as Chancy decides to take some lessons in love from a handsome hunk of a cowboy!

Eileen Wilks's latest, *The Wrong Wife,* is chock-full with the sizzling tension and compelling reading that you've come to expect from this rising Desire star. And so many of you know and love Barbara McCauley that she needs no introduction, but this month's *The Nanny and the Reluctant Rancher* is sure to both please her current fans...and win her new readers!

Suzannah Davis is another new author that we're excited about, and *Dr. Holt and the Texan* may just be her best book to date! And the month is completed with a delightful romp from Susan Carroll, *Parker and the Gypsy.*

There's something for everyone. So come and relish the romantic variety you've come to expect from Silhouette Desire!

Lucia Macro

Lucia Macro
And the Editors at Silhouette Desire

Please address questions and book requests to:
Silhouette Reader Service
U.S.: 3010 Walden Ave., P.O. Box 1325, Buffalo, NY 14269
Canadian: P.O. Box 609, Fort Erie, Ont. L2A 5X3

ELIZABETH BEVARLY
LUCY AND THE LONER

SILHOUETTE *Desire*™

Published by Silhouette Books

America's Publisher of Contemporary Romance

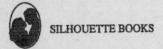 SILHOUETTE BOOKS

ISBN 0-373-76063-9

LUCY AND THE LONER

Books by Elizabeth Bevarly

ELIZABETH BEVARLY

is an honors graduate of the University of Louisville and achieved her dream of writing full-time before she even turned thirty! At heart, she is also an avid voyager who once helped navigate a friend's thirty-five-foot sailboat across the Bermuda Triangle. "I really love to travel," says this self-avowed beach bum. "To me, it's the best education a person can give to herself." Her dream is to one day have her own sailboat, a beautifully renovated older model forty-two footer, and to enjoy the freedom and tranquillity seafaring can bring. Elizabeth likes to think she has a lot in common with the characters she creates, people who know love and life go hand in hand. And she's getting some firsthand experience with maternity, as well—she and her husband welcomed their firstborn, a son, two years ago.

For my husband, David, who,
after twenty books, is still supportive,
still indulgent and still cooking.
I couldn't have done it without you.
Here's to twenty more.

And with much, much gratitude to
Captain George Meyers (AKA Roscoe) of
Chicago, Illinois, who, happily and with great humor,
answered an exhaustive list of questions about his fire-
fighting profession, and who added more than a little
color to the book as a result. Any inaccuracies that may
appear in the story do so because of my own
erroneously drawn conclusions.
Thanks, George!

One

Lucy Dolan woke slowly to utter darkness and discovered quickly that she was unable to breathe. A huge, heavy weight seemed to have settled on her chest while she was sleeping, and it had pushed the air right out of her lungs. When she tried to inhale, her breath leapt back out of her mouth in the form of a burning cough that seared her throat and coated her tongue with a foul taste. Another cough followed, then another and another, until she began to grow dizzy and rolled right out of bed.

Landing on the floor jarred her fully awake and afforded her some meager ability to catch her breath. But the air that passed through her lips tasted dirty and felt hot. Instead of reviving her, it made her head ache and caused her to feel oddly lethargic. As she reeled awkwardly over onto her back, she wondered why she couldn't see the hallway light that she always kept lit at night. Only then did she realize that what she was breathing wasn't air at all—it was smoke. Thick, black smoke that eclipsed the hallway light, burned her eyes and threatened to suffocate her.

Fire. Good God, her house was on fire.

When the recognition of that finally registered, her mind scurried into action. Unfortunately, instead of rehearsing an escape route that she'd never bothered to plan anyway, all Lucy could think about was Mack.

Mack. Oh, God. Where was Mack?

The last time she'd seen him, he'd been stretched out on the couch in the living room, the television still tuned to the Bullets game in its fourth quarter. He'd been sleeping soundly, but she hadn't had the heart to turn off the TV, knowing he preferred to doze in front of the flickering light. So she'd pulled the edge of the cotton throw over his feet to ward off the autumn chill, and she'd crept up to bed, knowing he'd join her there later when he awoke and realized she'd gone up without him.

She had to find him. She couldn't leave the house without Mack. If anything happened to him, Lucy would die herself.

In a distant corner of her brain, she recalled something from elementary school about how if your house was on fire, you should crawl along the floor, where there was likely to be more air, and touch any doors to check for heat before you opened them. Most of all, she remembered, you shouldn't panic. But when she rolled back over, the scratch of the rug against her belly made her remember something else, too. She remembered that she slept in the nude.

So much for not panicking.

She tried to get her bearings and forced all thought from her mind to focus instead on survival—her own and Mack's. She always discarded her clothes on the chair by the bedroom door before she went to bed, and—gee, what a coincidence— the door was also the best exit from the smoke-filled room. Certainly that was the direction she needed to pursue if she was going to find Mack.

Slowly and deliberately, keeping her breathing as shallow and steady as she could, Lucy clawed at the rag rug beneath her, pulling her body along the floor toward the chair. She fumbled around for a few seconds before her fingers lit on the boxer shorts and T-shirt that lay there in a crumpled ball. When she snatched the garments down to the floor, her hand skimmed against a soft patch of fur, and she remembered the tattered teddy bear who perpetually occupied that chair as if it were a throne.

She couldn't save much, Lucy thought as she reached up again, but by God, she would take care of the two things that mattered the most to her in the world. She was going to get Mack and Stevie the bear out of there. When all was said and done, they were all she had left in the world anyway.

It took her only a couple of seconds to struggle into her clothes, then, clutching Stevie savagely under one arm, she crawled out into the hall and immediately lost her way. She could tell neither where the fire was coming from, nor where the smoke was thinnest, nor could she detect any heat that might give her a clue.

Yet she knew she had to make her way downstairs. If Mack wasn't in bed with her, chances were good that he was still sleeping on the couch. If everything worked out the way it was supposed to, she would find him, rouse him, and they could flee through the front door together. Only problem was, by now she was so disoriented that she wasn't sure in which direction the stairs lay, let alone the front door.

It took her two tries and too many valuable minutes to find her way to the stairs. When she finally managed to locate them, she slithered like a snake, step by step, to the bottom. Toward the end she began to feel woozier and even more confused, and she bumped her chin hard on something when she lost her bearings.

For a moment Lucy simply lay sprawled on the floor at the foot of the steps, dizzy and disoriented, uncertain about exactly where she was. Her head was pounding, her mouth was dry and her chest felt as if it was going to explode. All around her was darkness and heat, and she didn't know which way to go.

Vaguely she heard a strange sound and registered it as the whisper of the fire consuming her house.

Funny how quiet that sound seemed, she thought as a buzzing swelled up from somewhere deep inside her brain. Her mind was reeling now, and her lungs felt as if they, too, were being eaten by hot flames. She'd always thought fire would be louder than this, hotter than this, faster than this. She didn't realize it would be so...so...so...

Somewhere in the house glass shattered, the odd tinkling sound seeming clearer than anything she had ever heard. Her hand clenched convulsively on the ragged bear she had managed to cling to, and she gripped it as fiercely as Arthur would have seized the Holy Grail, had he ever found it. But Arthur never had. Arthur had gone to his death never knowing the fate of that thing he'd sought so faithfully, so relentlessly, all his life.

Lucy didn't want that to happen to her. Stevie the bear was the only link she had to her own Grail, and she didn't want to lose him or the prize he signified to her. In some deep, delirious part of her brain, she vowed to herself that if she managed to get out of this thing alive, she'd go after that prize—her Grail.

Somehow, if she managed to get out of this thing alive, Lucy would find her twin brother.

But her thoughts as she fought off unconsciousness weren't for Stevie or her missing twin or the odd emptiness in her soul that had accompanied her all her life. Her only thoughts—indistinct and incoherent—were for Mack. Oh, God...she had to find Mack....

Boone Cagney heaved himself out of the cab of the bright red ladder truck, feeling, as always, that faint thrill deep down inside him where the little boy who'd always wanted to be a fireman still lived. Quickly, dispassionately, he surveyed the burning house.

Not as bad as some he'd seen, he noted as he immediately reached for his bunkers, but not much would be salvageable after the fire was out, either. With a competency and able-mindedness that had come with years of fighting fires, he donned roughly fifty pounds of protective gear—pants, coat, helmet and gloves. Finally, when he had his self-contained breathing apparatus in place, he forgot all about the fact that scarcely ten minutes ago, he'd been sound asleep, and he headed into the fray.

A handful of civilians mingled in the yards of neighboring houses, but he had no way of knowing yet if any of them were residents of the one that was on fire. Probably none of them were, because no one was acting hysterical—yet. Because it was just past 3:00 a.m., whoever lived here had more than likely been home when the fire broke out. The chances were good that they might even still be lying in bed overcome by smoke, oblivious to the fact that their house was burning down.

He made a quick survey of the grounds, noting there were no toys to indicate the presence of children, nor fences to indicate the presence of a pet. Which didn't necessarily mean that there weren't any, but it was a good sign. A pickup truck was parked in the driveway far enough back to be safe from the flames for now, one of those sporty models that weren't meant for transporting anything much heavier than a good-sized golden retriever. Even in the dark, Boone could tell the color was one of those weird mixes of pink and purple, so he guessed that at least one of the occupants of the house was female.

Although a good part of the structure had already been engulfed by flame, his practiced eye told him the source of the fire was probably somewhere in the basement, more than likely in the back. The aged garage, which stood independently of and behind the house, was also on fire, probably due to an errant spark from the burning building or stray bits of airborne, smoldering ash. Rolls of opaque black smoke bled from a number of broken windows around the base of the house.

While his colleagues advanced the hose lines, Boone went

to work on the ladders. As far as he could see, the flames were confined to the lower level of the house for now, but they would still have to be quick in their search of the second floor above the fire. He noted one window on the side of the house was open, in spite of the cool October night, and, determining it to be the most likely place to find a resident, he called to another firefighter and suggested they enter the house there.

Immediately after crawling through the window, he was surrounded by smoke, but his vision was still clear enough for him to make out a bed. An empty bed. Its covers were rumpled and kicked to the foot, however, as if someone had awakened and left in a hurry.

A quick search of the two other rooms upstairs revealed one to be a home office of sorts, with a personal computer on the desk whose screen saver still danced and glowed eerily through the dark haze of smoke. The other room was evidently a spare bedroom, unused if the still-made bed was any indication. Exiting that one, Boone nodded to his partner in the search, and the two men headed for the stairway at the end of the hall.

At the foot of the stairs, he found a woman. Initially, he thought her unconscious, but when he rolled her over, she groaned, and he could see that she was barely hanging on.

"Morgan!" he called into the radio he carried to alert the firefighters outside of the progress inside. "I got a woman just inside the front door—foot of the steps!"

"No other victims found," a voice crackled over the radio in response. "No one's been able to get into the basement— that's the source of the fire. But the neighbors said she lives by herself. Shouldn't be anyone else in there."

"Well, that's something, anyway," he said to himself, relieved that this rescue, at least, would be uneventful. The woman on the floor was small and slender, seemingly without weight, so he easily scooped her up into his arms.

He exited through the front door, and carried the semiconscious woman across the front lawn toward the street, then lay her effortlessly on the grass. When she groaned again, a sputtering cough erupted, and she flailed one hand in front of herself as if she were trying to physically grab hold of the fresh air. To help her out, Boone went back to the ladder truck to retrieve the oxygen they carried on all the rigs, returned to the woman and cupped the clear mask over her mouth.

As he monitored her breathing and waited for the ambulance, he noted the brown-and-black teddy bear she held clenched in one hand. It was threadbare in spots, ragged in others, and a fierce, hot fury gripped him at what her possession of the toy might mean. She coughed and sputtered some more, tears spilling freely from her eyes, but unable to wait any longer, Boone snatched the mask off her face and pulled her to a sitting position.

"Lady," he said, giving her a quick shake to help rouse her. "You're okay. But I need to know if there's anyone else inside the house."

A new series of rough, ragged coughs rocked her for a minute, and more tears rolled down her cheeks, leaving stark, clean streaks in the soot that smudged her face. Then she looked up and gazed at him with wide, panicked eyes, eyes that were so big and so blue, he nearly forgot for a moment where he was. Hastily, he brushed the odd sensation off and reminded himself that he had a job to do.

"Mack," the woman whispered hoarsely, the single word barely audible. She stared vacantly at the burning building for a moment, then riveted her gaze to Boone's with an intensity that shook him to his core. "Mack is still inside the house."

Great, Boone thought. Why was he not surprised? Her rescue had been too easy, too neat. Evidently she didn't live alone after all. Obviously her neighbors didn't know her as well as they thought they did. Or maybe she just had a boyfriend they didn't know about.

"Is Mack your husband?" he barked out, the roar of the flames behind them growing louder, threatening to drown out their voices. "Your boyfriend?"

She started coughing again, then stared at him, obviously still confused and uncertain. "My husband?" she finally re-

peated, her expression bewildered, those blue, blue eyes gradually sharpening their focus a bit. "No, I—I'm divorced. And
I don't have a…a boyfriend. Mack is my—" She seemed to
recall the gravity of the situation then, because she grabbed
his coat savagely and cried, "Mack! My God, he's still in
there!"

With one strong hand, she jerked Boone down until his face
was within inches of hers, and her eyes filled with tears again.
"You've got to get him out of there. Mack is all I have left.
He's…he's…" She began to cry in earnest then. "God, he's
only three years old! Please…you have to help him!"

Boone's entire body went rigid. "Where was he the last
time you saw him?"

"Asleep on the couch in the living room," she said, crying
freely now, her sobs blurring her words. "He was sleeping so
soundly, I didn't want to wake him when I went to bed, so I
just left him alone. I…I… Oh, no…"

Something hot and coarse knotted in Boone's belly. Once
more, he noted the teddy bear the woman clenched in the hand
that wasn't gripping his coat. He hadn't seen a child's bedroom, nor any other indication of a child's occupancy, save
the teddy bear in the woman's death grip.

But they hadn't made it down to the basement, he reminded
himself, a sick feeling gnawing at his belly when he remembered the radio announcement that the other firefighters hadn't
been able to make it down there. That's where her child's
room must be. Good thing she'd left him sleeping on the
couch, Boone thought. Otherwise the kid would have been a
goner.

Man, a kid, he thought wildly. There was still a kid in there.

"Where's your living room?" he demanded. "Where's the
couch he was sleeping on?"

The woman seemed to snap out of her stupor some, because
her next directions were offered with some degree of coher-
ency and a great deal of demand. "Turn left when you go
through the front door. The couch is on the far side of the
room."

Boone nodded. "Okay, we'll get him out. You stay put. Thompson!" he shouted out to one of the other firefighters nearest the front door. He heaved himself away from the woman, shoved his helmet visor back down over his face and began to race toward the burning house. "There's a kid inside! We're going back in for a kid!"

Boone had fought enough fires that watching his back was second nature. What other people might consider a terrifying situation was just another job for him to do. Usually. But when there was a kid involved, something inside him got anxious. Something inside him got scared. Something inside him got wary.

This time when he entered the house, it was with a single-minded intent to locate a three-year-old boy.

The general rule of thumb in his line of work was that where victims of fires were concerned, adults acted like dogs, and children acted like cats. While the former tended to run, the latter would normally hide. Boone hoped like hell this kid wasn't an expert at hide-and-seek. Otherwise, they were both going to wind up toast.

Left, he reminded himself as he passed over the threshold and into an incinerator. She told you to turn left.

When he'd entered the house the first time, the flames had been confined pretty much to the back of the house. Now, suddenly, there was fire everywhere. The smoke, too, impeded his progress, blinding him at times. Without wasting a moment, he motioned Thompson toward one side of the room, and Boone moved to the other, looking for a couch against the opposite wall, finding it exactly where she had said it would be.

But there was no child sleeping on it.

Terrific, he thought morosely. Who knew where the kid could have taken off to?

"Check across the hall," he told his partner. "But don't go far."

As Boone moved quickly forward to search the room, he

caught a quick movement from the corner of his eye, and, spinning quickly back around, saw that there was someone on the couch, after all. But it wasn't a child. Instead, a huge, black, malevolent-looking beast reared back on its hind legs, clearly terrified and slashing at the air with its claws.

Helplessly, Boone groaned aloud. A cat. He'd come back into a raging inferno to save a child, only to be obstructed now with the rescue of a cat. He hated cats. He really did. For good reason, too. And this one looked to be a real bruiser. Or flesh-eater, as the case may be.

An ominous creak sang out above him, a sound with which Boone was all too familiar. The upper floor was about to come down on top of him. He had maybe thirty seconds to get out before it did. Without even thinking about what he was doing, he completed his rushed search of the room and, satisfied the boy was elsewhere in the house, crossed to snag the cat, collect Thompson, and head for the front door. They'd have to come back for the boy through another entrance. They had no other choice.

When he was within inches of grabbing the big animal, it backed against the sofa cushion, flattened its ears angrily, and batted wildly at him with claws roughly the size of scimitars. Even with his hands well protected with heavy gloves, Boone halted before seizing the cat.

"You gonna give me a hard time, big guy?" he asked the growling beast, wondering why he was bothering, since he already pretty much knew the answer, and time was slipping by fast.

The cat hissed, spit, growled some more, flailed at the air, reared up on its hind legs as if to strike...then keeled over, quickly losing consciousness. Boone's eyebrows shot up in surprise. Okay, so maybe not the exact answer he was expecting, but it would make his job infinitely easier.

"A fighter to the end, huh?" he muttered as he scooped the animal up as effortlessly as he had its owner only moments ago. "I admire your spirit."

He tucked the cat into his coat and called out to Thompson,

and the two men turned to flee, barely making it out of the house before the floor above the living room crashed down in an explosion of pyrotechnics. The reverberation of the noise and the flash of heat at his back told Boone how close he'd come to being trapped. Wouldn't have been the first time, he reminded himself. Then again, did he really want to go through an experience like that again?

As he raced from the house into the chaos outside, he saw the woman he had carried to safety earlier being restrained—barely—by one of the other firefighters. Behind her, an ambulance with red lights tumbling through the haze of smoke stood ready to carry her to the hospital. But she'd obviously refused to make the trip until she knew the fate of her child, and Boone wasn't exactly surprised.

He could see that she had been watching for him to emerge from the house, and when she saw him, she catapulted forward. Her face was still streaked with black from the smoke, her short hair was matted to her forehead with perspiration and the water from the firehoses, her clothes were wet and filthy and clung to her like a second skin. But those eyes…

He had to force himself to look away. He'd never seen anyone with eyes that blue. And the soot on her face only made them appear that much more vivid. Her gaze penetrated him to his soul when he approached her. This was a woman who would never be able to hide her feelings, he thought. Her eyes, huge and round and thickly lashed, were the kind of eyes that a man would lose sleep over. Some men, anyway, he amended. Not him. He never lost sleep over anyone. Not anymore, anyway.

He was overcome with a sense of guilt and failure at having come from the house without her son, and could only watch helplessly as she kept moving forward, her gaze never leaving his, her pace never slowing. Her lips parted, but no words emerged. Which was just as well. He could already hear her accusing, panicked voice demanding to know why he'd come out of the house without her child. As she drew near enough to reach out and touch him, Boone withdrew the still-unconscious cat from his coat, to hand the animal off to one of his colleagues before returning for the boy.

But at the sight of the motionless animal, the woman halted in her tracks and fell to her knees. Then she buried her head in her hands and began to weep as if her heart were broken.

"Mack," she sobbed without looking up, as if she couldn't bear the sight of the unconscious beast. "Oh, Mack. You were too late to save him."

Boone gazed at her for a moment, completely dumfounded. Then, finally, he realized what he had done. He held up the cat. "This is Mack?" he asked incredulously.

The woman nodded and finally looked up at him, her eyes filled with tears. Her gaze dropped briefly to the motionless animal in his arms before returning to fix it on Boone's face. Then she began to cry freely again.

Boone could only stare back at her for a moment, so entranced was he by the piercing intensity of her gaze. Finally, he shook the hypnotic sensation off and managed to ask, "Mack is your cat? I went back into that inferno to save your *cat?*"

She nodded mutely as she lifted a hand to gingerly stroke one of the cat's dangling paws. "Oh, God, he's dead. You couldn't get him out. Oh, it's all my fault." She buried her face in her hands again, and began to cry even more helplessly.

She was terrified that she had lost her cat, Boone realized, the same way a mother feared the loss of her child. Her whole body shuddered with every sob that erupted from inside her, and her dark head moved helplessly back and forth. Before he could stop himself, he threaded his fingers through her short hair, stroking the damp tresses until she looked up at him again. Gently he urged her head backward and pushed her bangs back from her forehead.

"No, lady, don't cry," he said softly, swiping at a fat tear that tumbled down her cheek. The cat twitched in his arms when he did so. "It's okay. Your cat's still alive. He's even starting to come around. He just needs oxygen."

She gazed at him levelly, those blue, blue eyes incredulous.

"He's alive?" she cried. "You got him out okay? He's not dead?"

Boone shook his head and turned to make his way quickly to the oxygen he had used earlier, with the woman following only inches behind him, scrambling three steps for every one of his. "He was unconscious, but he's starting to rouse," he called over his shoulder as he went. "And he does need oxygen."

He settled the animal gently on the grass beside the teddy bear the woman had left there, picked up the same plastic mask she had worn, and dropped it over the animal's muzzle. Then he shed his gloves and began to slowly stroke his hand over the cat's thick, wet fur, rubbing it lightly under the chin and cupping a hand over its rib cage to feel for its heartbeat.

Okay, he conceded as he watched the helpless creature lay still and half-conscious. Maybe cats weren't so awful after all. This one, at least, had shown some spirit and had a strong will to survive. Boone had to respect that. It was something he identified with greatly. Survival was his reason for living, after all.

"His pulse is strong," Boone told the woman. "Just give him a minute."

Stooped down on his haunches, he was more than a little aware of her hovering over him. She stood close behind him, her knees pressing against his back and her hands settled on his shoulders. Obviously, she had no qualms about getting familiar with strangers. Boone had to force himself not to physically shake her off. He *did* have qualms about getting familiar with strangers. And not just ones with huge, haunting blue eyes, either.

But now that the immediacy and danger of the situation had passed, he was able to consider her a little more fully. Still holding the mask over the cat's muzzle, he turned around to look at her.

Man, she was a mess. Soot-covered, water-damaged, shivering from the cold and damp, she was bedraggled enough to qualify for urchin status. In spite of her appearance, however, there was something compelling about her. Boone wasn't sure what, but something in her struck him as being just as spirited, just as much a survivor as her cat was. Had he not gone in after the animal, he was quite certain she would have done so herself, barefoot and unprotected as she was. Even at the risk of killing herself, she would have gone back to retrieve that cat.

He wasn't sure he could say the same thing about himself. He was a loner, and he couldn't imagine caring so much for someone that he would place that someone's well-being above his own. Sure, part of what he did for a living was save lives. But hey, that was his job.

He was still thinking about that when the animal beneath his fingers began to twitch again. Then the cat began to thrash. Then it began to scratch. Before he could stop it from happening, the big black beast bared its claws again and tore a thin red line down the entire length of Boone's thumb.

"Ow, dammit," he growled.

Now he remembered why he hated cats. One of the reasons, anyway. He stuck his thumb into his mouth and sucked hard before pulling it out again to inspect the damage. While he was contemplating his wound, the cat disappeared from his grasp.

"Mack!" the woman behind him cried, bending over Boone so quickly and powerfully that she nearly knocked him sprawling to the ground. She yanked the cat up into her arms and buried her face in its fur, then started making kissy noises against its neck and ears. She glanced down at Boone, her expression concerned. "Is it okay to take the mask off now?"

He nodded, still sucking on the side of his thumb. Bastard cat, he thought.

The woman carefully removed the oxygen mask and held her pet aloft. "Oh, Mack," she said, lowering the cat again to rub her nose playfully against his, the kissy noises becoming more pronounced.

Boone tried not to gag.

"I'm so glad you're safe," she went on, cuddling the animal in her arms exactly the way one would a newborn baby. She turned to gaze anxiously at Boone again. "He *is* going to be okay, isn't he?"

At his nod, she expelled a shaky breath, her eyes filling with tears again. "You're sure?" she asked anxiously. "I mean, he's not going to have brain damage or anything, is he?"

"He'll be fine," Boone assured the woman, inspecting the damage to his hand again, wondering if he could say the same about himself. He hoped the beast's shots were all up-to-date.

The woman dropped to her knees beside Boone and threw her free arm around him, to hug him close. Her next word was muffled against his neck, but it seemed to be, "Thankyouthankyouthankyouthankyouthankyou."

Boone peeled her arm from around his neck, more than a little uncomfortable with her gesture. He wasn't a hugger and never had been. He didn't like huggers and never would. Hugs were just so...so... An involuntary shudder wound through him. He just wasn't into that touchy-feely stuff. As quickly and discreetly as he could, he pushed himself away from the hug and moved out of range of any further public displays of affection.

Seemingly oblivious to his rebuff, the woman stood and began to nuzzle and hug the cat again as if it were a child. And oddly, the cat seemed to tolerate her gestures with no problem at all. Boone could only shake his head in wonder at them both. In spite of the cool morning, he was wringing wet with perspiration, thanks to the heat from the flames and the heaviness of his protective gear. So he unsnapped his helmet and removed it for a moment, to wipe the sweat off his face and out of his eyes before returning to fight the fire.

He was still running his hands briskly through his damp, dark blond curls when he heard the woman say, "Everything's going to be okay, Mack. Just you wait and see."

Boone was about to replace his helmet on his head when, as if cued by her comment, what was left of the house behind them came crashing in on top of itself. They spun around in shock and surprise to find flames thoroughly consuming her home. Boone eyed the woman warily, uncertain how she was going to take this new development.

Although she'd cried freely when she'd thought her cat was dead, her eyes were dry as she watched her house burn, her expression completely impassive. It was almost as if she didn't care, he thought, wondering why not. Almost as if—

Her legs buckled beneath her then, and she fell hard onto her bottom beside Boone. She snuggled the cat close to her chest, nuzzling his head with her cheek. Then, still staring at her burning house, and almost as if she wasn't even thinking about what she was doing, she felt around on the grass with her free hand until she located the teddy bear she'd been carrying with her. And she clutched that to her heart, too.

All Boone could think was that he hoped she had some heavy-duty fire insurance. Because the only thing she was going to have left in the world was the truck parked in her driveway and literally the clothes on her back.

And a recalcitrant tomcat.

And a ragged teddy bear.

"Sorry, lady," he said softly. "But it looks like you've lost everything."

She shook her head, squeezing the cat and the teddy bear close to her heart. "No, I haven't," she told him with a sad smile. "Everything I need, everything that matters most, is right here with me. Thanks to you."

"Don't thank me," he said with a negligent shake of his head. "Just doing my job."

"You have no idea what you just did."

Her words were cryptic, but he decided that was a result of her shock at seeing her possessions go up in smoke. He shrugged off the comment and replaced his helmet, ready to rejoin the battle. Of course, he conceded, the battle now was essentially lost—her house was toast. There was nothing more he or his colleagues could do except make sure the fire was confined to the one building until they finally extinguished it.

"What's your name?" he heard the woman ask as he turned to leave her.

"Boone," he replied automatically. "Boone Cagney."

"I owe you, Boone Cagney," she told him. "I owe you big. And I always pay my debts. Always."

He turned to look at her and shook his head, shoving his hand into a heavy glove. "You don't owe me jack, lady. Like I said. Just doing my job."

"Lucy," she murmured softly.

He turned to look at her and nearly lost himself in those spectacular blue eyes. "What?"

She was still holding the cat and the bear, and for some reason, Boone was overcome by a massive wave of protectiveness. Which was really crazy. Protecting people was his job. It wasn't something he wanted to do in his personal life, too.

"My name isn't 'Lady,'" she told him, her gaze steady and dry-eyed. "It's Lucy. Lucy Dolan."

"Well, Lucy Dolan," he said, forcing himself to look away from her amazing eyes, "you need to get on that ambulance and go to the hospital, just to be on the safe side. And you might want to get your cat to a vet, just to be sure. But you don't *owe* me anything."

"Oh, yes I do," she countered. "And you can't imagine how huge the debt is. I don't know how I'm going to repay you, but I will. Somehow, some way, I'll settle the debt." When he turned to look at her again, she nodded sagely and vowed further, "I promise you that, Boone Cagney. I promise you that."

Two

Lucy nudged a black, sodden, still-smoldering lump with the toe of her borrowed sneaker, and wondered what the sooty blob had been before succumbing to the fire. The teapot her mother had ordered from England and loved so much? The box that had held her father's fishing lures? The piggy bank full of quarters her grandmother had given her for her twelfth birthday? It was impossible to tell.

She tilted her head to the right to contemplate the object once more, squeezed her eyes shut to fight back the tears that threatened, and inevitably replayed in her mind the events of the night once more.

So much of what had happened was just a blur of unrecalled chaos now, and she guessed there were some things she would never quite fully remember. She supposed she was lucky neither she nor Mack had been hurt beyond a little smoke inhalation and the jerky handling necessary to save their lives. Ultimately, confident she was perfectly all right, Lucy had declined the complementary ride to the hospital that was evidently the consolation prize when one's house burned to the ground. But she'd made an appointment with the vet for Mack this afternoon.

Perfectly all right, she repeated to herself. Oh, sure. She was perfectly all right. Just fine and dandy. Hey, she wasn't going to let a little something like losing all her worldly possessions spoil her day. No way. She shivered and tried not to think about how badly this whole episode could have turned out if it hadn't been for the big blond firefighter.

What was his name again? she wondered. Oh, yeah, Boone Cagney. Boone Cagney who had emerged from smoke and fire to carry her and Mack to safety, then hopped back up on his big red truck to disappear into the night. Without a word, without a trace, without even realizing the magnitude of what he had done.

Lucy sighed deeply and stared at the sparse remains of her house. Gone. Everything. Just like that. The track and field hockey trophies from high school that had lined her bedroom windowsills like soldiers. The airplane models she had built so passionately as a child. Her favorite pair of blue jeans— the ones it had taken four full years to get faded just the way she liked them.

Odd, the things people felt wistful about once those things were gone. And now Lucy had nothing.

Actually, that wasn't true, she reminded herself. As she had told Boone Cagney, she did still possess the two things that were most important to her in the world—Mack and Stevie. And, of course, there was the truck she'd just bought a few months before and that she'd never been able to fit in the cluttered, cramped garage. But her house, her furniture, her clothes, and everything else she had ever owned—all the physical trappings that made Lucy Dolan Lucy Dolan—all that was gone forever.

She hugged the teddy bear tighter to her, rubbing her chin over the worn spot on top of his head that had become worn by that same gesture for thirty-four years, and wondered how

she was going to take care of Mack—not to mention herself—
now that she had nothing else left.

"Lucy?"

She turned at the sound of her name to find her next-door
neighbor, Mrs. Palatka, wringing her arthritic hands in worry.
It was she who had made Lucy put on the sneakers some time
ago, but the older woman had been unable to get her young
neighbor to do much more in the way of self-preservation.
Lucy was still wearing the clothes she'd managed to throw on
before making her escape, but she was only now beginning to
realize that the T-shirt and boxer shorts were damp and cold
and offered no protection from the chill morning air. In spite
of that, she scarcely noted the goose bumps mottling her flesh.

"Come to the house and have some breakfast, dear," Mrs.
Palatka said. "You need something to warm you up."

The white-haired, warm-hearted woman looped a surprisingly sturdy arm around Lucy's waist and squeezed hard. Mrs.
Palatka hadn't changed out of her night clothes yet, either, and
beneath her winter coat fluttered a red flowered muumuu emblazoned here and there with big purple letters that spelled
out, Aloha from Waikiki! Coupled with her huge, purple,
fuzzy bedroom slippers, limp from the morning dew, she
looked almost as much the part of a refugee as Lucy did.

"Come on," she said again. "You're going to catch your
death out here. You need a hot shower and some hot food.
And you can borrow some of my clothes until you get settled."

Recalling that Mrs. Palatka's wardrobe consisted almost ex-
clusively of synthetic Capri pants and fluorescent halter tops
for the full-figured gal, Lucy battled a smile. "That's okay,
Mrs. P.," she told her neighbor. "I keep my work clothes in
the truck. They'll do for now."

Wordlessly, she collected a few things from the cab of her
pickup, then allowed herself to be led to the house next door.
She listened passively to the soothing words her neighbor offered about thank God no one had been hurt and it was a good

thing Lucy had insurance and tomorrow was another day and everything would work out fine, just wait and see.

She put herself on automatic pilot and let Mrs. Palatka ply her with hotcakes and sausages and coffee. Then she mechanically showered, letting the hot cascade pelt her back, watching with an odd melancholy as the black, sooty water swirled down the drain. She pulled a faded green, hooded sweatshirt over her head and stepped into a pair of equally faded, baggy denim overalls, donned her work boots, and felt a little better. Only when Lucy was seated on her neighbor's couch with nothing more demanding to do than stare out into space did the enormity of her situation finally register.

She had no place to go. No one to turn to.

Except for Mack, Lucy was completely alone in the world. She was an only child, having been adopted as a toddler, and her parents had died within a few years of each other by the time she was thirty-one. With only a handful of cousins she'd met maybe two or three times in her life scattered on the other side of the country, Lucy essentially had no family left. And the Arlington, Virginia, house where she'd grown up, the only house she'd ever really known, was nothing now but a pile of ash.

All she had left was Mack, who had pretty much been her only family for more than three years—ever since he'd shown up as a shivering, soggy handful of skin and bones at her back door, following a monstrous thunderstorm the morning after her mother's funeral.

Lucy had taken his timely appearance to be a sign. As silly as it might sound to others, she'd always had the feeling that Providence had given her Mack to love and care for, because she'd had no one else left for that after her mother's death.

That was why she owed such a huge debt to the firefighter who had rescued him. By running back into a blazing house, Boone Cagney had saved the only living creature in the world Lucy needed and loved, the only living creature in the world who needed her and loved her in return. Without Mack, her life would be hollow, joyless and lonely. Boone Cagney had saved Lucy's family. He had saved her life.

She inhaled a broken, battered sigh and released it in a shudder of breath. From nowhere Mack jumped up onto the couch and bumped his head against her elbow, then nuzzled close before curling up in her lap. Lucy smiled and rubbed her hand along his back and under his throat, and the thrumming of his steady purr reassured her some.

As long as she had Mack, she told herself, everything would be okay. Somehow, some way, she'd put her life back together again. She'd just have to force herself to focus on the future and not dwell on the past. Piece of cake, right?

She sighed furtively and decided not to think about it for now. What consumed her thoughts instead was the huge debt she owed to Boone Cagney. And although Lucy prided herself in the fact that she *always* paid her debts, the settlement of this one eluded her. Everything she owned was gone. Her financial savings were meager at best. Whatever she received for her house from the insurance settlement was going to have to buy and outfit a new place for her to live.

All she had was a tattered teddy bear whose inherent value would be useless to anyone but her, and Mack, with whom she would never part, no matter how grave the debt. She simply had nothing to offer the big, blond firefighter who'd saved Mack's life, she realized morosely. Unless, of course, she wanted to give him herself. But why would he want something like that? No one else ever had.

The hand stroking Mack's back gradually slowed, then stilled altogether as a hazy idea rooted itself in her brain. Actually, she thought, that just might work. There *was* a way Lucy could repay Boone for everything he had done for her. There *was* something she could give him that would settle the debt in some small way.

She *could* give him herself. Sort of.

Now all she had to do was figure out how to wrap herself up all nice and neat and make him accept her small token of gratitude. Unfortunately, Boone Cagney didn't seem like the kind of man who was open to receiving gifts, whether they were owed him or not.

"So what do you think, Mack?" she asked the cat who had moved into her lap, tucked his legs up under himself, and curled his tail around his body quite contentedly.

Mack opened one eye, clearly disinterested, then closed it again, sighed with much satisfaction and purred louder.

Lucy thought some more as she rubbed Mack behind the ear. "I guess if he's not the kind of guy who accepts things easily," she murmured, "then I'll just have to be a bit more persuasive than usual."

Mack grunted in his sleep, though whether the sound was one of agreement or dissension, Lucy couldn't tell.

"That's okay, Mack," she said softly to the slumbering animal. "I'll take care of everything. You just be yourself."

Boone had finally managed to slip into a restless slumber when a rapid knocking at his front door awakened him with a start. Jerking his head up from the pillow, he squinted at the blurry green numbers on his clock, then swore viciously when he realized he'd only been in bed for a little over an hour. With another muffled curse, he collapsed back onto the mattress and mentally willed the intrepid intruder to go away.

But the pounding only reverberated through his house again—louder this time. So he sighed his resignation and rolled out of bed, then stretched lethargically before scrubbing two hands through his hair. Because he was expecting to send his uninvited caller on their way right quick, he didn't bother to put on a shirt, and instead padded barefoot across the bedroom, wearing only a pair of faded navy blue sweatpants.

Man, it had been a bitch of a night, he thought, rubbing a knot at the base of his neck. It was a terrible thing to watch a person's house—a person's *home*—go up in flames along with all their worldly possessions. He supposed he'd never get used to that part of the job. The only thing worse than seeing something like that happen was seeing something like that happen to someone you cared about personally.

The thought stopped him dead in his tracks. *Whoa*, he instructed himself carefully, *rewind*. Cared about personally? He couldn't even remember the name of the woman whose house had burned last night. How the hell could he care about her?

The pounding erupted again, so he shook the thought off and returned to his slow progress down the hall. Prepared for an unwanted solicitation or an unexpected delivery, he jerked the front door open with a growl, only to find that the woman he had been thinking about only seconds ago had materialized from his ruminations and stood on the other side.

Although it was common enough for women to cross the street just so they could walk by a fire station, Boone couldn't recall a single incident where one had actually come to a firefighter's house. Although now that he got a better look at her, he decided it might not be such a bad tradition to start.

"Hi," she greeted him with a bright smile. "Remember me?"

For a moment he couldn't say a word. He could only stare into those compelling blue eyes that had lingered in his thoughts until sleep had claimed him. No, he suddenly remembered, that wasn't exactly true. Even in sleep, those eyes had haunted him.

"Yeah, sure I remember. You okay?"

She nodded anxiously but said nothing to confirm her condition for sure.

Boone nodded vaguely in response and forced himself to pull his gaze away from her eyes. Inevitably, though, it roved relentlessly over the rest of her. Cleaned up, he noted, she looked a little sturdier than she had the night before. Cleaned up, she looked a little heartier. She looked older, too, probably near his own thirty-six years, and much less fragile and commanding of care. Last night, she had seemed close to crumpling into a hopeless, helpless heap of despair. But now...

Now, he realized, in spite of the baggy, masculine, obviously borrowed clothing that hung on her body like sackcloth, she actually looked quite...fetching.

Although her bangs were long—nearly down in her eyes—

her black hair was cut shorter than his own. The style might have been boyish had it not topped such utterly feminine features. Her lashes seemed even darker than her black hair, a stark contrast to the pale blue of her irises. Her cheekbones were well-defined and stained with pink, though Boone knew without question that the color didn't result from any manufactured cosmetic. Her full lips, too, were blushed with color, though again, he could see that heightened emotion, and nothing more, caused the flush.

Dropping his gaze lower, he also saw that she bore a nasty bruise on the left side of her chin that reached to her mouth and swelled a small portion of her lower lip. Without even thinking about what he was doing, he curled his forefinger lightly against her mouth and brushed it gently over the injury. Vaguely he noted the warm breath that danced over his fingers. Vaguely he marveled at how soft her skin was. Vaguely he realized how much he wanted to touch her in other places, to see if they were warm and soft, too.

Her lips parted a mere breath, but her pupils expanded to nearly eclipse the blue of her irises. Only when he noted her reaction did Boone fully understand the intimacy inherent in his gesture, and the strangely erotic path his thoughts had suddenly begun to follow. He yanked back his hand with the speed of a viper and shoved it down to his side. Then he tried to meet her troubled gaze with as much indifference as he could fake.

He was about to say something else—although he couldn't quite remember what—when she seemed to throw off the odd spell that had descended and snatched his hand back up to inspect it. Until then, he had forgotten about the jagged red line that rent his thumb from the cuticle nearly to his wrist.

"Oh, my God, did Mack do that to you?" the woman asked, stroking the pad of her thumb delicately over the wound.

Boone jerked his hand out of her grasp, uncomfortable with the way his skin warmed under her touch. But all he said in response was, "Yeah."

She reached for his hand again, and when he snaked it back

to his side, she looked positively dashed. "I am so sorry about that. Mack would normally *never* scratch someone. Really. He was just scared last night. He wasn't himself."

Boone expelled a dubious sound. "Yeah, I'm sure. Just tell me his shots are all up-to-date."

"Of course they are," she assured him. "Honest, he really is the sweetest creature in the world. If you got to know him, you'd realize that."

Boone tried to keep his voice impassive when he replied, "Thanks, but I think I'll pass."

"I mean it. If you want—"

"You look a little battered yourself," he interrupted, lifting his chin to indicate the contusion that marred her otherwise flawless complexion. "Did you have that checked out by a doctor?"

She shook her head, then touched the bruise and her lower lip with considerably less care than he had, working her jaw as if testing the damage. "It wasn't necessary. It's not as bad as it looks. I think it must have happened when I was coming down the stairs," she added. "I don't really remember much of what happened. One minute I was waking up in bed, the next I was standing in the yard holding Mack, watching my house burn to the ground."

"It's not unusual for people to experience that kind of thing when they've been through something like that," Boone told her.

She nodded quickly, and he began to understand that the action wasn't so much born out of her agreement with anything he said as it was her complete uncertainty about the situation.

"The insurance guy has already come by, can you imagine?" she hurried on. "I had no idea they'd be that efficient. Unfortunately they're not quite as efficient at issuing checks. He could only give me an advance for now. Still, it's better than nothing, right? And they already found the source of the fire, too," she added, her obviously forced cheerfulness beginning to fade. "It was my clothes dryer. Of all things..."

She chuckled, but the sound was strangled and uneasy and accompanied by a sparkle of moisture in her eyes that she hastily swiped away with the back of one hand.

Although he couldn't imagine why he cared, Boone heard himself ask, "Is there anything you need? Do you have someone to stay with? Family in the area?"

She sniffled and shook her head. "No. My folks passed away a few years ago, and I'm an only child." She hesitated for a moment before amending, "Actually, I do have—"

She physically shook off whatever she was going to say, and as quickly as she'd changed the subject before, she changed it again. "The advance will cover anything I'll need right away—clothes, food, that kind of thing. I've got a room at the Arlington Motor-on-Inn. Don't know how long I'll have to stay there, though."

Boone nodded, his mind reeling at the dizzying wealth of information she'd imparted in that one quick announcement. And for some reason, he felt oddly cheated that there wasn't some small thing he could offer to do for her. The reaction was more than a little strange. He hadn't wanted to do something for somebody in a long time. Not since he'd offered himself heart and soul and lock, stock and barrel to his fiancée—or rather, his ex-fiancée—and received a good, swift kick in the teeth for a wedding present.

"Mind if I come in?" the woman asked, squashing the usual bitterness that generally rose with memories of Genevieve before it could rise to the fore. She held up her other hand to display a fast-food-issued cardboard caddy that held a bag of doughnuts and two plastic cups of coffee. "I went by the firehouse to look for you, but the guys there said you got off at eight and had already gone home. They also said you wouldn't mind if I stopped by, as long as I brought you some coffee and doughnuts when I did."

She grinned brightly, but it was clear that she was still none too certain about the response she was likely to receive from him.

"They, uh...they told me where you live," she added, her

smile falling somewhat. She seemed to think it was very important that he have that information. "I, um…I didn't even have to ask for your address. They wrote down directions and everything. One of them even drew me a map."

Boone gazed at her for a minute, trying to picture the scene at the station as it must have unfolded. Twelve randy firefighters ogling an attractive woman with eyes the color of a tropical sky. Yep. Must have been interesting.

"They told you I like coffee and doughnuts for breakfast?" he finally asked, somewhat mystified about that particular part of the story.

She bit her lip a little anxiously. "Actually, um…what they said was that you'd love to have me this morning, because you always like a little something, uh—" She cleared her throat indelicately, and the pink in her cheeks turned to red. "They said you like something, um, hot and sweet…in the morning. I just naturally assumed what they were talking about was—"

"I see," he interrupted her before she could finish. Oh, yeah. He was going to have a little chat with his brothers down at the station. Pronto.

Reluctantly Boone stepped aside for her to enter, and she sailed past him on a breeze redolent of Ivory soap. The scent was appropriate for her. She seemed like the clean-cut, eat-all-your-vegetables, go-to-church-every-Sunday kind of woman. In other words, not at all his type. Not anymore, anyway.

"Look, lady—" he began as he closed the door behind himself.

"Lucy," she corrected him over her shoulder. "Lucy Dolan. Where's the kitchen?"

"Lucy," he repeated obediently. "Keep walking. At the end of the hall turn right."

He hesitated for a moment, then halfheartedly followed her to the room in question and found her making herself way too comfortable way too quickly. Without asking for permission to do so, she searched his cabinets until she located his dishes in the one by the sink, and carried two plates to the small oak table. Then she unpacked two doughnuts—presumably one for him and one for her—and took a seat at one of the chairs. Too tired and bemused to protest, Boone pulled out the chair opposite her and sat down, then removed the plastic lid from the cup of steaming, fragrant coffee and brought it to his lips for a sip.

Fortified by even that small gesture, he lifted his doughnut for consideration before taking a bite. When he swallowed, he said, "This is about that debt you said you owe me last night, right?"

She nodded as she bit into her own doughnut, but was obviously too polite to speak with her mouth full.

"I told you that you don't owe me anything," he said. "But it was nice of you to bring me breakfast. Thanks."

She swiped at a dusting of powdered sugar on her upper lip, then licked a scant dribble of jelly from the corner of her mouth. The gesture, although more than a little stirring—for him, anyway—seemed nervous, but he couldn't imagine what she might have to feel uneasy about.

"Actually," she said, decorously hiding her mouth behind her hand as she spoke, obviously embarrassed by his scrutiny, "this *is* about that debt, but you can't possibly think that I'd consider a bag of doughnuts sufficient repayment."

"Why not? All I did last night was my job. And I didn't even do that well enough to save your house. Or much of anything else, for that matter."

"You did a lot more than save my house," she told him. "You saved my family. You saved me."

"I saved your cat, you mean. You were almost out the door by the time I got there."

She reached across the table and covered his hand with hers. Well, as much of his hand as she *could* cover with those child-sized fingers of hers. They were good hands, though, he noted. Sturdy with short, blunt nails and seemingly no special care. They were working hands, plain and simple. Boone liked that. Genevieve's hands had looked like something out of a diamond advertisement. He'd never been able to understand women who seemed to make a career out of grooming their hands as if they were thoroughbred horses.

When he looked up at her face again, Lucy was studying him with an intensity that made him uncomfortable. And as much as he wanted to look away, he found that he just couldn't.

"Like I said," she told him softly, "you saved my family."

Her cat was her family? he wondered. Her *cat?* Hell, even *he* wasn't *that* alone in the world. Not really. Not like that.

He pushed the thought away and focused on Lucy instead. His gaze drifted to the angry blue discoloration on her chin again, and he wished he could have arrived at the scene of the fire sooner—before she had taken her spill. Nothing should mar skin that beautiful, he thought, especially something like a bruise.

Then he reminded himself that thinking such things had gotten him into trouble in the past. And he could no more afford that kind of trouble now than he had been able to then. Playing the sucker once was bad enough. No way was he going to get taken in like that a second time.

"I saved your cat," he reiterated.

"And me, too," she reminded him. "You carried me to safety."

"I just happened to be the one on the scene," he said, explaining away the action before she could interpret it as heroic. "I was just doing my job. Anyone else in my situation would have done the same thing. It was no big deal."

She shook her head in obvious disappointment, then withdrew her hand from his and wrapped it around her cup again. For a moment she only stared silently down into its dark depths. Then she said softly, "That's okay. I don't expect you to understand about me and Mack."

When she looked up at him again, a stark sadness glittered in her eyes. "But the fact of the matter is that last night you ran into a burning house—a burning house, for Pete's sake—

to save my cat. A cat that means more to me than you can imagine. And for that I owe you. Big.''

Boone wondered if she'd feel the same way if he told her the reason he'd returned to that inferno to retrieve her cat last night was because he'd thought he was going back to save a child. What would she say if he confessed that had he known what he was risking his neck for was a cat, he probably would have just sat out on the lawn and let the damned thing be toasted into a kitty waffle?

Ultimately he decided it was probably better to keep that information to himself. It was one thing to brush off a woman's concern for a debt that didn't exist. It was another matter entirely to make her want to strangle you with her bare hands.

"And I'm going to pay you back for what you did," she told him again. "I promise you I am."

When Boone Cagney said nothing in response to her assurance, Lucy fidgeted a bit in her chair. Hoo boy, she thought. She'd really managed to get herself into it this time. Last night, in the chaos and panic of the moment, she hadn't bothered to pay much attention to her rescuer's looks. But now, seated here in the picture of domestic bliss at his kitchen table, sharing doughnuts and coffee as if it were something the two of them did every morning, she realized he was a lot more attractive than she had recalled.

Not handsome, really. His features were too irregular, too unconventional for that. But definitely very attractive. His heavy-lidded eyes gave him a deceptively calm appearance, but there was a fire burning in their green depths that was too vivid, too bright, too *hot* for her comfort. His thick, dark blond curls might have been considered tousled on another man, but on this man, their dishevelment seemed more the result of anarchy.

His mouth, however, was what drew her attention most. *Lush, mellow* and *evocative* weren't words Lucy would normally use in relation to a man who seemed so hard and unrelenting, but they all sprang immediately to mind when she gazed at Boone Cagney's mouth. It spoke promises of incomparable sensuality without him ever having to utter a word.

She lowered her gaze when she realized she was staring at him. Then she felt her face heat up at the blatant hunger that hummed in her midsection at the sight of his naked chest and the rich scattering of dark blond curls that swirled from his shoulders to his belly and beyond. Lucy had never much gone for the overdeveloped, muscle-bound type. And although Boone Cagney was clearly a man who worked out and took care of his physique, he was no bulging neckless wonder like so many body builders seemed to be.

His form was solid, but in no way overdone. Swells of well-defined musculature corded his torso, and sculpted curves of sinew whipped around upper arms that were truly things of beauty. His forearms, too, were lean and hard with muscle, and an involuntary tremble shook her when she realized those arms were what had carried her to safety the night before.

Figures she'd only be semiconscious during something like that, Lucy thought wryly. That was the way her luck always seemed to run. Then again she wondered if any woman would remain at all coherent when arms like those pinned her to a body like that.

Had she remembered how attractive he was, she might have reconsidered the proposition she was about to make. But she was resigned now to what she was going to do. Because she simply could think of no other way to repay him for all that he had given her.

"You don't have to pay me back," he insisted in response to the promise she scarcely recalled making.

That was another thing about him that made her nervous. That voice. So low and husky, so slow and sexy. He rolled over every word leisurely, thoroughly, as if each one were an erotic vow of the most carnal variety. It was the voice of a man who would be quick to seduce and slow to satisfy. Every time Boone said something, it sent a ripple of hot delight buzzing right through Lucy's libido.

She ignored his assurance to the contrary and told him, "Here's what I'm going to do."

"Lady...Lucy—" he immediately corrected himself when she opened her mouth to do it for him "—like I keep telling you, it's not necessary to pay me back for anything. Okay?"

Instead of succumbing to his tone of command, Lucy hurried on before she had a chance to change her mind. In a rush of words so quick they almost sounded like one, she told him, "Here's the deal. I'm giving you myself for one month."

When the only response she received was a silent stare of complete incomprehension, Lucy tried again. "I'm yours to do your bidding, at your beck and call, for four weeks."

But still he seemed not to understand.

Finally, in an effort to make it as clear as possible, Lucy took a deep breath, met his gaze as levelly as she could and told him, "For the next thirty days, Boone Cagney, I'll do whatever you tell me to do. Because for the next thirty days, I'm going to be your slave."

Three

―――――

Not even the slightest flicker of acknowledgment lit his features when she outlined her intentions. Instead, he lifted his cup to his mouth for another idle sip of coffee and continued to gaze at her in that drop-lidded, maddeningly level way that made her want to reach over, take his hand lightly in hers and whisper, "Hey, big boy, why don't you take me to the Casbah?"

"Did you hear me?" she asked instead, her voice sounding hollow and hesitant, even to her own ears. "I said I'm going to be your slave." When he still remained silent, she elaborated further, "For one full month, starting today, I'll do whatever you tell me to do."

He bit his lower lip thoughtfully for a moment, his eyes never leaving hers, and gradually her offer seemed to register. "My slave," he finally repeated blandly.

She nodded, but said nothing more.

"For one month."

She nodded again.

"Starting today."

"Uh-huh."

"I see."

Then he sipped his coffee negligently, his expression thoroughly bored, as if hers was the kind of offer he received every day. Then again, who was Lucy to say that he *didn't* receive offers of enslavement from women everyday? She wouldn't be in the least bit surprised to discover that there were scores of women just begging him to tie them up in his basement. Or wherever. And why did that realization bother her?

"That's all you're going to say?" she asked, surprised she could keep her voice steady. "'I see?'"

He sipped his coffee carelessly again. "What am I supposed to say?"

She scrunched up her shoulders for a moment, then let them drop. "You're supposed to take me up on my offer."

"Well, since you couldn't possibly be serious about your offer, why should I give you a serious response?"

"Who says I'm not serious?"

He rose out of his chair and leaned forward, bringing the naked upper half of his body over the table until his face was within inches of hers. His hooded eyes no longer seemed sleepy and disinterested, Lucy noted. On the contrary, they suddenly came alive with something indecent and incandescent.

"You're offering to be a slave for a month to a man you don't even know," he said in that soft, slow voice, "and you consider it a serious offer?"

Well, when he put it like *that,* she thought, it did kind of sound a little...well...different from what she had originally intended.

"I mean, *slave,*" he repeated, pushing himself even closer to her, his voice growing quieter, more sinister, as he spoke. "That word just conjures up all kinds of...interesting images, doesn't it?"

Lucy leaned back in her chair, but the action did nothing to distance her from his interrogation. "Um, now that you mention it, I guess it *could*, if—"

"Just what kind of woman," he interrupted her, "would allow herself to be *enslaved* by a man she barely knows?"

Instead of seating himself in the chair that he'd occupied directly across the table, he plummeted into the one immediately next to Lucy and scooted forward. Then he propped one elbow on the table and settled his chin in his hand, and he leaned in close—very close—to her again.

He smelled of pine soap and wood smoke and something else she couldn't identify, the combination intoxicating and irresistible. She closed her eyes and inhaled deeply of his scent, holding her breath in her lungs for a long moment before releasing it in a ragged whisper of air.

"Hmm, Lucy?" he murmured softly. "What kind of woman makes an offer like the one you've just made?"

When she opened her eyes again, she found that he had moved closer to her still. If she'd wanted, she could have tilted her head just the tiniest bit and kissed him without the slightest effort. But of course, she reminded herself absently, he was actually little more than a stranger, and she didn't want to kiss him. Not really.

Not yet.

The odd realization ruffled her, and she stammered out her reply. "One who...uh...who has a big debt to pay," she finally managed to get out. "A really, really big debt. Huge, in fact," she added emphatically, still shaken by her wayward thoughts. "Really...very...um...huge."

Boone nodded, his gaze still boring into hers with a heat unlike anything she'd ever experienced before. "A *huge* debt, huh? Wow. I can only imagine what it's going to take to repay a debt that big." He paused a deliberate beat before adding, "Boy, can I imagine."

He seemed to be pondering something that she was pretty sure he had no business pondering. Lucy observed him through narrowed eyes, wondering about the look he threw her as the wheels turned in his brain. Curiosity warred with speculation on his face, both traits inflamed by a kind of murky desire. For one heated, heady moment, she felt herself responding to it. For one heated, heady moment, a curious, speculative, not-so-murky desire wound through her.

Until she stamped it out and extinguished it thoroughly. There was absolutely nothing sexual about her offer, she reminded herself. Nothing. Nada. Zip. Zero. Zilch. Just because a man had the most come-hitherest bedroom eyes she'd ever seen, and just because the thick swirls of hair strewn rampantly across his chest and torso absolutely commanded a woman's touch, and just because she couldn't quite dispel the hazy, half-remembered vision of being carried to safety in those incredible arms, and just because it had been a long, long time since any man had made her this jumpy and aroused, and just because his mouth was so…so…wow, so—

Lucy gave herself a good mental shake and reminded herself of the task at hand. Just because of all those other things, it didn't mean she had to succumb to Boone Cagney. Being his slave for a month was one thing. Being his *love* slave for a month was a different matter altogether.

Although, now that she thought about it…

Stop it, she chastised herself. Don't be that stupid. Again.

Lucy had practically enslaved herself to her ex-husband during the six years they'd been married. She'd done everything within her power to please Hank Dolan, only to have him toss her out on her keester, anyway. You couldn't trust men. She knew that. You could do everything exactly the way they wanted it—whether *you* wanted it that way or not—and they still weren't satisfied. She'd be an idiot to put herself through something like that again.

"I, um," she began. But for some reason the words she needed to say wouldn't come. "That is…I mean…" She sighed unevenly and tried again. "I don't think you're…"

She shifted clumsily in her seat and tried to look him in the eye as steadily as she could, then dropped her gaze to the fingers she twisted restlessly together on the table. But when that just made her more nervous, she forced herself to look at his face again.

"You, uh…you don't seem to be taking this offer in the spirit it's intended," she finally told him.

"Oh?" he asked mildly. "And just what kind of spirit is it intended in?"

Lucy knew the only way she was going to get through this was to stop staring at him. As long as Boone Cagney and his chest were in her line of vision, all she could do was wonder if his lower half was as intriguing as his upper half. So she darted her gaze around his kitchen, letting it ricochet off everything but him.

"When I say I'll be your slave for one month," she began again, "what I mean is that I'll do chores for you. Things around the house that need doing that you haven't had the time or inclination to do yourself."

"Chores," he repeated, his voice belying nothing of what might be going on in his brain.

She continued to stare over his shoulder at the calendar on the opposite wall as she spoke, noting that it was running two months late. "Uh-huh. Chores. You know. I'll wash your car, rake your leaves, do your grocery shopping. Bring you breakfast in the morning on my way to work," she added lamely, "or fix your dinner on my way home. Things like that."

When she looked at Boone again, he seemed to have his mind on something other than breakfast. His chin was still settled firmly in one hand, and the curious fire in his eyes continued to blaze wickedly.

"Will you make my bed?" he asked.

She chewed her lip anxiously, unable to tear her gaze away from that odd heat that seemed to grow brighter with every passing moment. "Uh, yeah. Sure. I can do that."

"Every morning?"

She hesitated for a moment, then told him, "If that's what you want."

He opened his mouth to say something else, seemed to reconsider and snapped it shut again. Then he leaned back in his chair and folded his arms across his chest, his posture displaying better than words ever could, "Game over."

"It's not necessary," he said simply.

For some reason, though, Lucy had the feeling he wanted to say a lot more. "Of course it's necessary," she insisted.

He shoved the chair back from the table with a loud scrape and stood, then crossed the small kitchen in a few quick strides. He turned to face her again, leaning back against the counter, gripping its edge with his palms, his long legs extended before him. His posture was casual, but his expression was carefully controlled.

"I appreciate your wanting to do this," he said, "but I don't want you to."

"But I owe you, don't you understand?"

He started to protest again, but Lucy cut him off by standing abruptly enough to send her own chair toppling over. Ignoring it, she covered the same distance he had just crossed, stopping directly in front of him. She had to tilt her head back significantly to study him face-to-face, but it was imperative that she make him understand.

"I have a debt to pay," she said simply. "And I always pay my debts."

Well, all but one, she reminded herself, that old specter of insufficiency jabbing a cold finger at the back of her brain again. She'd never paid her parents back for adopting her. Even after she'd turned out to be in no way what they'd expected or wanted, they'd kept her, anyway.

What they'd wanted was a daughter—a soft, cuddly little creature in pink ruffles and curls, who would take ballet lessons and play the piano and sing in the Sunday school choir. Someone who wouldn't speak unless spoken to, and who would concede daintily when opposed. That's what her parents had wanted when they set out to adopt a little girl.

What they'd wound up with in Lucy was a fighting little hellion who'd given the neighborhood boys a run for their money. No one at school—male or female—had ever been able to beat her. Not at games, not at sports, not in fights. In spite of her parents' endless efforts to restrain her, Lucy had refused the mantel of "traditional female." She'd liked and excelled at athletics, machine arts and all things boyish. And she'd never looked pretty in pink.

And seemingly not a day had gone by when Lucy hadn't heard about what a disappointment she was. Nor could she recall too many times when her parents missed an opportunity to remind her of how grateful she should be that they'd taken her in—and kept her—in spite of her many shortcomings.

Lucy owed them more than she would ever be able to repay them, they often told her. And they'd been right. She never had managed to become the kind of daughter they really wanted. And now that they were dead, that debt would remain unpaid in full.

But not this one. Lucy wasn't going to carry around another unsatisfied obligation for the rest of her life. Especially when the debt she owed Boone was one that she had the ability to repay with fairly little effort.

"It's not a debt," he insisted, snapping her out of her troubling reminiscence.

"It *is* a debt," she countered.

Boone stared down at Lucy, knowing there was a lot more going on here than she was letting on. He didn't know why she should find it so necessary to free herself from an obligation to a total stranger—an obligation that didn't even exist, as far as he was concerned—but for some reason, she just couldn't let it go.

Nevertheless, the last thing he needed or wanted was someone like Lucy Dolan invading his space, invading his house, invading his life. He was a loner, pure and simple, someone who thrived on solitude and cherished his self-induced isolation. He liked his house quiet, and he liked his life undisturbed.

And even in the scant time he'd spent with her, he could see that Lucy was the kind of woman who would never be quiet and who would always disturb, in one way or another. He didn't need or want such a disruption in his life.

"Forget it," he told her, wanting to put an end to this whole bizarre situation right now. It was imperative for his survival to hustle her out of his house—his life—once and for all.

"But—"

He curved a hand over her shoulder and squeezed hard, holding his breath so he wouldn't drown in the treacherous depths of her eyes. "You just got burned out of your house," he pointed out gently. "You need to be worrying about doing things for yourself right now, not for someone else."

She actually looked wounded by the fact that he wasn't going to hold her to her so-called debt, Boone marveled. She actually seemed disappointed that she wouldn't be rearranging her life for a month to pay back some crazy obligation that she didn't even have.

Then it occurred to him that maybe that was the whole point to her offer. Maybe the source of her insistence to meddle in his life was some subconscious manifestation of her unwillingness to face what had happened to her. Maybe by focusing her energy on disrupting *his* life, she wouldn't have to be thinking about putting her own back in order. Which was all the more reason to insist she not go through with her silly offer of enslavement.

Not that he wasn't beginning to warm to the idea of having a beautiful woman at his beck and call. Actually, he amended, maybe *warm* was too tame a word. *Burn* might be more appropriate. Or *seethe* perhaps. Or *strain at the bit,* even. He was certainly beginning to strain against something.... He shifted his position a little and stifled the groan that arose when his loose sweatpants seemed to suddenly grow tighter.

"But I have to pay you back," she insisted, her voice lacking the enthusiasm it had boasted before. "I have to."

"Go home, Lucy," he said quietly, hoping to put an end to the discussion once and for all.

"But—"

"Go home."

She chuckled once, but the soft sound was in no way happy. "I don't have a home," she said quietly.

Boone mentally kicked himself for his gaffe, but didn't quite know what to say in response. Finally Lucy saved him the trouble by sighing heavily and knifing her fingers through her hair.

"Okay, I'll go," she said. "But this isn't settled. I owe you my family and my life, and I intend to pay you back, whether you like it or not. That's a promise, Boone Cagney. It's a promise."

And with that she spun on her heel and made her way out of the kitchen without a backward glance. The hardwood floor in his hallway squeaked and creaked with every step she took, and all Boone could think was that the sound was her way of punctuating her assertion somehow.

And he knew right then that he wasn't rid of Lucy Dolan. Not by a long shot.

His suspicions were confirmed the following evening when he returned home from his other job. Firefighters' shifts consisted of twenty-four hours on duty, during which time they literally lived at the station—eating meals there and sleeping there—and forty-eight hours off, when they returned home.

For that reason most firefighters had side jobs they performed when they weren't on duty. In Boone's case, he taught lifesaving classes at the local Y. Together, the two jobs afforded him a life-style that was, if not luxuriant, at least busy enough that he didn't have to think about a lot of things that he didn't want to think about.

Like Lucy Dolan, for example. Like Lucy Dolan's eyes, and how they were empty of secrets and full of warm, wistful need. Like Lucy Dolan's hands, and how soft and comfortable and right they'd felt when they'd covered his own that morning. Like Lucy Dolan's mouth, and how he wanted so badly to—

Boone groaned inwardly as he pulled into his driveway and found it already occupied farther up by her pinkish-purple pickup truck. He should have known better than to think he could forget about Lucy so easily. In spite of his numerous and vigorous efforts to chase each and every errant thought about her from his head—efforts that had been largely ineffective, anyway—he could see that his memory was about to be refreshed. Uncomfortably, annoyingly, lustily refreshed.

When he emerged from his car, he immediately detected the smell of smoke. Barbecue grill-type smoke, coming from the direction of his backyard. It was accompanied by a proliferation of raucous jazz music, enlivened by lots and lots of brass. He sighed his resignation, scrubbed a hand quickly over his face to wipe away any wistful, wanton expression that might still linger there and went to confront his slave.

He found her bent over a barbecue grill that appeared to be brand new, brushing a marinade redolent of garlic and peppers over a variety of chicken parts and two good-sized steaks. She held a glass of wine in one hand—the one that wasn't covered by an oven mitt shaped like a huge lobster claw—and she danced around a bit in time with the music.

This evening she was wearing clothing that fit much better than her duds of the previous day. Manufacturer-faded blue jeans hugged her trim hips and legs, and a cropped red sweater played a fascinating game of hide and seek with the creamy skin of her lower back. Accessorizing the ensemble was an apron emblazoned with the command, Kiss the Cook.

Beyond her, stretched out on a lounge chair like a pasha, was her cat, Mack, clearly a lot more comfortable than Boone was at the moment. Mack saw him before Lucy did, and the animal's relaxed posture immediately turned aggressive. The big beast stood and eyed Boone warily, and his tail fuzzed up into something that looked almost like an animal itself. Then he arched his back and expelled a long, low growl, a menacing, disembodied sound more suited to a werewolf or a sociopath than to a house pet.

The howl alerted Lucy, who spun around and smiled at Boone with an expression that was every bit as welcoming as her cat's display was repellent.

"Hi," she said, her voice utterly at ease, as if their strained exchange yesterday morning had never occurred, and as if it were perfectly normal for her to be at his house, grilling out in his backyard. "I was wondering when you'd be home."

Reluctantly, because he was in no way convinced he would be safe turning his back on the animal, Boone shifted his attention from Mack to Lucy. He approached her slowly, cautiously, still wondering about her presence in his yard after he'd repeatedly told her to go away. She didn't *look* like a madwoman, but she had been through a lot in the past couple of days, and you never could tell how people were going to react to tragedy.

"Well, gee, since I never mentioned it to you," he said carefully, "simply because—silly me—I had no reason to think you'd be here, I don't suppose you could have been expected to know when I'd be home, could you?"

She gave his question some thought, then nodded. "I guess you're right. Is steak okay for dinner? There's chicken, too, if you'd rather have that. And potatoes under the coals."

He halted his approach a good two feet before her—well out of swinging distance, should she become...unpredictable—and smiled as inoffensively as he could. She turned the chicken pieces with a pair of shiny new tongs, pierced a steak with a shiny new fork and continued to hum along with the music as if there were nothing out of the ordinary in her usurpation of his turf.

"Looks like you've been spending some of your insurance money," he said.

She smiled. "Yeah. The grill is the first thing I bought. Kind of ironic, huh? But I just love cooking out. At least, I did. Before...um...before...well, you know."

Her face clouded some, and once again Boone wanted to kick himself for reminding her of her loss. But she recovered quickly, turning a chicken leg as if she were concerned about little more than whether he wanted regular or extra crispy.

"Lucy?" he finally said.

Instead of looking at him, she reached for a bottle of wine that was chilling in a cooler on the ground. Then she poured a second glass and handed it to Boone. "Hmm?"

He ignored the wine and asked, "What are you doing here?"

She stared at him as if he were a complete lunatic. "Fixing your dinner, of course."

"Why?"

"Because I'm your slave, and that's what slaves do." She nodded toward the glass in her hand. "Here. You look kind of tense. A glass of wine will help you unwind."

"No, thanks."

She lifted her lobster hand to her forehead. "Of course. How silly of me. Red goes much better with steak."

"No, thanks," he repeated firmly.

"You don't want wine?"

He tried not to sound too bitter when he reiterated, "No. Thank you. I don't drink."

She blinked at the absolute conviction in his voice, then said, "Oh. Okay. I'll just, um…uh…" She picked up her own, nearly empty glass, and poured the remnants of her wine on top of his. "There. I don't usually have more than one or two, but—" she shrugged "—I don't have to be anywhere for a while."

Boone didn't like the sound of that at all. "Why not?"

"Because, like I said, I'm your slave for a month." She spread her arms open wide in playful surrender. "Do with me what you will."

He had actually begun to entertain some ideas in that area—most of them shamelessly salacious—when a low, level growl from behind them sounded again. Quickly he spun around to find Mack perched on the very edge of the lounge chair, looking as if he were ready to pounce. The ebony beast was eyeing him as if Boone, and not the steaks, was really what was on the menu tonight. Then the big beast licked his chops with a bright pink tongue, and if Boone hadn't known better, he would have sworn the animal grinned. Menacingly.

"Uh, Lucy, about that cat of yours…"

"Mack?" she asked innocently. "He's harmless. He's just kind of moody tonight. I don't think he's quite recovered from the fire. But don't worry. He'll behave himself. He's a good boy."

As if cued by her assurance, the cat leapt to the ground and made a mad dash for Boone's ankles. He braced himself for the impact, expecting Mack to claw and crunch his lower extremities into hamburger, and was surprised when the animal began to curl around and through his legs instead, almost as if he were trying to be nice to him.

"See?" Lucy said. "I told you he's a sweetheart once you get to know him."

Again, as if he had been simply waiting for that false reassurance from his owner, the cat sank his teeth into Boone's shin. Hard. Even through his blue jeans, the sting of those fangs hurt. A lot.

Boone yelped and jumped backward, slamming against Lucy, who nearly bumped into the hot grill. He grabbed her before her body made contact, pulling her close without even thinking about what he was doing. Then he glared down at Mack, who twitched his tail once and walked away, looking very, very bored with the new developments.

"What happened?" Lucy asked, sounding a little breathless.

"That damned cat bit me."

She made a face. "Oh, he did not."

Boone gaped back at her, incredulous. "He did, too. He was winding around my ankles, and for no reason at all, he just bit me."

"Oh, that wasn't a bite," she said with a laugh. "That was a love nip. He does that sometimes when he gets overly affectionate. It means he likes you."

Boone expelled a dubious sound. "That was no nip—it was a taste. He wants *me* for dinner."

"Don't be silly. One of the steaks is for him."

Certain he'd misunderstood, Boone asked, "You make a habit of feeding your cat steak?"

She waved him off with the tongs. "Of course not. Mack only gets steak on special occasions."

Lucy had intended to elaborate on that, but found herself

incapable of coherent speech when she suddenly realized exactly how precarious her position was. Not because she stood only inches away from a hot metal grill, but because she stood even closer than that to a much hotter, harder-than-metal man.

He seemed to be going a little soft, however, she thought when she looked up at Boone, although obviously not cooling in any way. His eyes suddenly had a glassy look to them, and his hands leisurely stroked her back as if he were taking a not-so-quick inventory of her ribs and vertebrae. She waited for a moment to see how long he intended to continue, and when he seemed in no hurry to conclude his investigation, when he in fact began to move his entire operation lower—a bit lower than Lucy found comfortable, or rather, lower than she knew she *should* find comfortable—she tightened her grip on his sweater and tried, discreetly, to push herself away.

But instead of letting her go, Boone seemed to want to draw her closer. She began to wonder if he even realized how intimately entwined they had become, so idle and unfocused were his caresses. First his hands seemed content to skim open-palmed over her back and shoulders. Then his fingers crept around to her front and strummed lightly along her ribs. But when one hand curved L-shaped under one of her breasts and began to inch upward, Lucy began to suspect that maybe Boone's focus was more fully pinpointed than she'd initially thought.

For one wild moment her curiosity—and something else she decided she'd rather not identify—got the better of her. For one wild moment she almost talked herself into letting nature take its course and letting Boone do whatever he wanted to do. She was, after all, his slave. But eventually, thankfully, reason stepped in.

Or rather, Mack stepped in. Stepped in and started to curl around Lucy's ankles before giving her a love nip on the shin she wasn't likely to forget anytime soon. And the tingle that shimmied up her leg as a result was all she needed to remind her that she really had no business being embraced in such a way by a man she scarcely knew, even if she was his slave.

Especially if she was his slave.

"Um, Boone?" she finally managed to say, hoping she only imagined the mousy little squeak that seemed to overtake her vocal chords.

The hand below her breast had the decency to halt in its tracks, but the one on her back continued to trace lazy circles as he replied, "Hmm?"

"I, um...I think I've got my balance back now."

He sighed with much contentment and dragged both of his hands to her waist, where his thumbs skimmed against her bare torso and seemed more than a little anxious to dip into the waistband of her blue jeans. "That's good."

A little explosion of heat and fire ignited everywhere he had touched her. Lucy closed her eyes, inhaled a deep breath and forced herself to say, "So, uh...you can, um...let go of me now."

The hands at her waist began to creep upward again, this time dipping beneath the cropped hem of her sweater, until his flat palms opened over her rib cage, just below her breasts. The caress had Lucy's heart hammering wildly against her breastbone, and helplessly, she felt her eyelids flutter closed.

When she opened them again, Boone was staring down at her silently, and a slow stain of red was rising up his throat to darken his face. "Oh, right. Right." His words were almost as jerky as his movements when he took a few steps backward and swiped his hands fitfully over his jeans. "Just wanted to be sure you didn't get burned."

Too late for that, Lucy thought. Way too late for that.

"Thanks," she managed to mumble. "I appreciate it."

He cleared his throat a few times with more than a little difficulty. "So..." he began again. "What's that wrapped in foil?"

She was grateful for the change of subject, however awkward, and followed his errant gaze to the tightly wrapped foil packages on the grill. "Cabbage rolls."

He made a face that would have been comical had Lucy not

still been so agitated by the sudden tension that seemed to have sprung up between them. "I hate cabbage," he said.

"Oh, you'll like it the way I fix it. With bacon and garlic and onions..." She smiled, hoping her expression was less anxious than she felt. "Trust me."

"Lucy, you have to stop this."

When she braved a glance up at him, he inhaled deeply, then drove his hands through his hair in what she was beginning to realize was his way of indicating his complete and utter frustration. He stared back at her for a moment, then, without further comment, he strode forward. He plucked the tongs out of her grasp and gently tugged the lobster claw pot holder off her hand.

"Go home, Lucy." Too late, he seemed to remember that she was, in effect, homeless. He squeezed his eyes shut, cleared his throat roughly and tried again. "I mean...go back to the motel and get some rest. Take care of yourself, not me. I'll be just fine."

Indicating that *she* wouldn't be, Lucy thought morosely.

Clearly, Boone didn't intend for this to go any further. And frankly, she had no idea what to do. She had to pay him back for saving Mack's life. But she didn't want to do it at the risk of becoming a nuisance. She'd been a nuisance before. And it was no fun. So, resigned to the knowledge that she was just going to have to try another tack where Boone Cagney was concerned, Lucy reluctantly nodded.

"I'll go. But you might as well enjoy dinner. I don't have anyplace to put the grill for now, anyway. I'll just come and get it after I've found a place, if that's okay."

He started to say something, then evidently changed his mind. She could almost see him switching gears as he said, "Um, look, this is no way to thank you for cooking my dinner for me. You went to all this trouble..." He sighed fitfully. "Why don't you stay and join me? Then you can go ho—" He clenched his jaw tight for a moment. "Then you can go back to your motel."

She brightened some at that, but knew she was still far from reaching his capitulation where the whole slavery thing was concerned. Still, this one concession had to be a point in her favor, right?

"Okay," she agreed, with as much cheerfulness as she could muster. She couldn't help noting that he seemed disappointed by her easy agreement, and she wondered if maybe she'd been too rash in calling the victory hers just yet.

"You're going to love this," she added, donning the big lobster claw again. "This marinade is a secret recipe that's been in the family for years...."

Four

Okay, so she could cook circles around Julia Child, Boone thought, as he gazed down at his empty plate some time later. That didn't mean he wanted her coming around every night to fix his dinner for him. Grudgingly he recalled that he hadn't enjoyed a meal that much since…well…

Actually, now that he thought about it, he supposed he'd never enjoyed a meal quite that much. Then again he normally just nuked something prepackaged in the microwave and ate all alone standing over the kitchen sink. He'd never been cooked a meal by someone who knew what they were doing. Nor had he ever sat across the table from someone who had eyes as blue and a mouth as sexy as Lucy Dolan's. Nor had he ever encountered anyone who drove a conversation quite the way she did.

Which actually shouldn't have been any kind of endorsement. The woman flew from topic to topic faster than the spread of a gasoline fire, the focus of her verbal assaults covering everything from local politics to lawn care to what a shame it was that Tony Curtis hadn't won an Oscar for *Spartacus* to how she'd spent her summer vacation. Some of her segues had made Boone's head spin. In spite of that, he'd hung on her every word.

"Coffee?" she asked him now, holding up his coffeepot to punctuate the question.

And that was another thing. In three short hours, she'd completely taken over his house. She had set *his* table with *his* dishes, and filled *his* refrigerator with leftovers. She'd scooped *his* coffee into *his* coffeemaker, and set out *his* sugar bowl and *his* milk.

So why did Boone feel like *he* was the guest here?

And why was he tolerating a cat in his bed? he wondered further. Because that's precisely where Lucy's damned cat was at the moment. Completely uninvited, Mack had trotted into the house right on her heels when she'd brought the steaks in, and after wolfing his down nearly whole—peeved, no doubt, because he hadn't been able to kill it himself—had run straight to Boone's bedroom upstairs. When Boone had followed him up, Mack had leapt up to *his* bed—to the side where Boone always slept—had curled up on *his* pillow and had gazed at him with huge green eyes as if daring Boone to come and get him.

Boone had actually taken a step forward to roust the obnoxious beast, only to hear that low-throated, unearthly growl erupt again. And he'd thought maybe, just maybe, a cat snoozing on his pillow wasn't worth losing a hand over.

This whole evening had just been too bizarre for words.

"Yes, thank you," he said, sounding perfectly normal in spite of that. "Coffee sounds great."

Lucy smiled and poured them each a cup, then heaped enough sugar to gag an ant farm into hers. "You sure you don't want any pie?" she asked him. "Sorry it's not homemade, but it should still be good."

He shook his head, more out of an utterly warped sense of reality than a decline of her offer. Actually, though, he was way too full to even think about something like dessert.

She seemed to misinterpret his reason for saying no, however, because she told him, "Next time I'll bake you one myself, I promise."

"No, Lucy, there's not going to be a next time," he replied quickly, wanting to get that straight right off the bat.

But she didn't seem to be listening. Instead, she was looking at his kitchen cabinets. "You know, a few coats of paint would really brighten this place up. And it wouldn't take any time at all."

"Oh, no, you don't," he said. "You are *not* going to paint my house."

She threw him a solicitous smile. "But all the rooms are so dingy. It doesn't look as if it's been painted in—"

"No, Lucy," he stated emphatically. "No."

She flattened her mouth into a tight line, but didn't press the issue. "Don't get me wrong—I do like your house," she said instead. "It's a lot like the one where I grew up."

Although he couldn't imagine why he was asking—certainly not because he was interested—Boone heard himself inquire, "And where would that be?"

She looked at him blankly for a moment, then clarified, "It was the one I lost to the fire."

He had lifted his coffee to his lips, but replaced the mug on the table with a muffled thump when the magnitude of her loss hit him. "You'd lived in that house all your life?"

Surprisingly her expression was more wistful than painful. "Actually I lived somewhere else until I was eighteen months old, but…" Her voice quieted and trailed off as she spoke, as if her memories had overtaken her words.

"But what?" he asked.

Her gaze returned to his, and she seemed to reconsider before talking about whatever she had been thinking about. "Nothing. Never mind." She sipped her coffee in silence for a moment, then said softly, "Can I ask you something?"

"Sure."

Pensively she traced idle circles in the wood grain on the table, her expression gradually becoming a little dreamy. Her voice, too, seemed to soften some when she asked him, "What do you think would be worse—to die before you've had a chance to do all the things you want to do, or to live and have there be nothing left that you want to do?"

It was, to say the least, not the kind of question he would have expected out of the blue on the heels of what had otherwise been a fairly companionable dinner exchange. Then again, he was beginning to understand that with Lucy it would probably be wise to always expect the unexpected.

"That's some question for after-dinner conversation," he said, uncertain how he should answer. "Why are you asking?"

She shrugged. "I don't know. I've been thinking a lot since the fire about what I should be doing with my life. If circumstances had been different, I could have died that night never knowing about a lot of the things I want to know about."

Something twisted inside of Boone at her easy, matter-of-fact discussion about her own possible death. And all he could say in response was, "You didn't die, though."

"But I could have," she countered.

"Lucy—"

"I mean, think about it," she said, interrupting him. "The human body is a pretty fragile creation. Between illness and accidents and foul play, it takes almost nothing to kill a person."

"Yeah, but the human body is also responsible for building things like the Great Pyramids, and waging and surviving more than a few wars, and creating and sustaining life. To me, that's not the work of anything fragile."

On the contrary, he mused, that whole life-generating business in particular was a pretty mind-boggling accomplishment. And why did something he'd scarcely contemplated before suddenly threaten to completely overrun his thoughts?

Lucy nodded slowly, clearly considering what he'd said. "I guess that's true, too."

She sipped her coffee once more, then seemed to pull herself out of her reverie. When she smiled at him, he noted again the bruise on her lower lip, and something inside him coiled tight. He supposed she *had* come uncomfortably close to dying in that fire. In another time, another place, she might have.

"Sorry," she said, "didn't mean to get so philosophical on you."

Boone slowly released a breath he'd been unaware of holding and asked, "Then why did you?"

She shrugged again. "Like I said, I've just been thinking a lot since the fire."

"About what?"

"About things I should have done by now but never did."

Again, he had no idea why he was curious, but he asked, anyway. "Such as?"

She gazed down into her coffee, instead of looking at him, when she replied. "Such as finding my family."

Once again she'd made a remark that utterly confused him. "I thought you said you didn't have any family, that your parents passed away a few years ago."

"They did. I just…" Again, she hesitated, as if she were unwilling to discuss the very subject she'd brought up herself.

"What?" he asked.

With no small amount of frustration, he was beginning to realize that the more he learned about Lucy Dolan, the more complicated she became, and, dammit, the more he wanted to know about her. Why? He had no idea. There was just something about her….

Lucy couldn't begin to imagine what had come over her to be revealing her deepest, darkest secrets to a virtual stranger. There was just something about Boone that made her want to open up to him, something that made him very easy to talk to. In spite of his constantly assuring her that he wanted nothing from her, there was something about him that drew her to him almost irretrievably. Whether he meant to or not.

"I have a brother," she heard herself blurt out, wondering when, exactly, she'd decided to reveal that.

His expression remained impassive, and it took her a moment to realize that he couldn't possibly appreciate the magnitude of her statement. Although she'd been convinced for years that her twin brother existed, and that she hadn't simply manufactured or imagined the faint recollections bouncing around in her brain, she'd never once verbally acknowledged it to anyone—even herself.

And now that she'd spoken of her certainty aloud, she had no way to take it back. It was out in the open now, for the entire world to hear.

"I'm sorry," Boone said, "I must really have been half-asleep when you came over yesterday morning, because I remember you saying you were an only child."

"I am an only child," she replied automatically, having uttered the fact so many times in her life.

"Then how could you have a brother?"

Lucy sighed heavily and knifed her fingers through her hair. Why on earth had she brought this up? she wondered. Especially with someone like Boone, who would probably never understand? It was only because of the significance of today's date, she told herself. It was only because of the odd sensations that overcame her at some point on this day every year.

It was only because today was her birthday.

"It's a psychological thing," she said with a sad, half-felt smile. "Or maybe it's a psychic thing." When she saw his confusion turn to utter bewilderment, she chuckled unhappily and further amended, "Or maybe it's just plain psychotic, I don't know."

He continued to study her, and she took some small comfort in the fact that he didn't run screaming from the house to warn the neighbors that some lunatic had tried to hold him hostage and force-feed him manic delusions.

Instead he only said, "You, uh…you want to talk about it?"

She shook her head. "It's so bizarre, I doubt you'd understand."

"Try me."

What was the use? Lucy thought. It was pointless to try. Over the years she had attempted to explain to a few of her closer friends the unusual ritual in which she unwillingly participated every year on her birthday. And never once had any of them understood. They'd always just nodded politely and thrown her looks one might reserve for oh, say…a prehistoric sea monster rearing its head from the darkest depths of a Scottish loch.

In spite of her misgivings, however, she began without preamble, "My parents adopted me when I was eighteen months old. I don't have many memories of my life prior to that, but I do recall having a twin brother. I remember sharing a crib with him, and I remember the two of us playing together."

He eyed her curiously. "Are you sure about that?"

"Absolutely sure," she told him. "My parents—my adoptive parents, I mean—told me I didn't have any birth siblings. They said if I did, they would have adopted them as well as me."

She dropped her gaze to the tabletop and picked restlessly at an errant leftover crumb. "Mom and Dad weren't able to have kids," she added softly. "They wanted a bigger family. I was never quite enough for them. For some reason, though, they, um…they were never able to adopt again."

Actually she knew full well the reason her parents had never adopted any more children. They'd never tried. Once they'd realized how badly their gamble on Lucy had played out, they hadn't been willing to risk adopting yet another child who would be nothing but a major disappointment.

"So what happened to your brother?" Boone asked.

She was grateful he didn't press the last part of her revelation. Her inadequacies as a daughter were something she'd rather not have to explain. It was far preferable to have him questioning her sanity than to have him knowing how badly she'd failed to be the offspring her parents had wanted.

"I assume he was adopted by another couple," she said. "Back then, I don't think adoption agencies were all that concerned with keeping families together. For all I know, my parents were never told I had any birth siblings. I have no idea where my brother is now."

When she braved a glance up at him again, Boone was

leaning back in his chair with his arms crossed resolutely over his chest. He appeared to be thinking hard about something, though whether he was questioning her account or had moved on to another matter entirely, she couldn't tell.

"Have you ever thought about hiring a private investigator?" he asked. "Or registering with one of those family search agencies that reunite people separated by adoption?"

She dropped her gaze and went back to worrying the crumb on the table. "I've thought about it."

"Why haven't you?"

She lifted one shoulder halfheartedly, then let it drop. "Because..." she began. But she couldn't bring herself to finish.

"Because why?"

She continued to focus on the crumb, instead of Boone or her troubling thoughts, when she replied, "Because...what if I found my brother—or even my biological parents for that matter—and they didn't..."

"What?"

Lucy expelled a restive breath of air, then looked up at him again. "What if they didn't...want me?"

Boone didn't know what to say. Not want her? Not *want* her? Who in their right mind wouldn't want Lucy? Hell, he'd *wanted* her virtually since the moment she'd shown up at his front door yesterday morning. Well, maybe not wanted her as a family member, he conceded, and certainly not forever, but the idea that someone wouldn't want her was unthinkable.

Unable to help himself, he spoke his thoughts out loud. "Why wouldn't they want you?"

She dropped her gaze back down to the table again and shrugged once more. But she said nothing in response. Her reaction was puzzling. Boone couldn't conceive of a single thing that would make a woman like her think she would be unwanted.

Except for maybe some guy who kept telling her to go home all the time.

He pushed the thought away. Surely she didn't misconstrue his need for being alone as having anything to do with her.

Maybe the fear of being unwanted was something all adopted people experienced. Then again, how could he possibly know? And why, dammit, was he expending all this energy worrying about it, when Lucy Dolan's situation in life was absolutely none of his concern?

He sighed and leaned forward, settling his elbows on the table. "I doubt very seriously your family wouldn't want you," he said softly.

She appeared to weigh his words carefully, but when she responded, she seemed to be talking more to herself than to him. "Well, there is that feeling I get every year on my birthday," she said quietly.

Although he wasn't sure he wanted to know, Boone asked, "What feeling?"

She still seemed to be preoccupied with herself rather than him when she explained, "The feeling that someone is out there thinking about me—trying to get in touch with me."

"I beg your pardon?"

Seemingly unable to tolerate sitting still, she rose hastily and began to gather their dishes, carrying them to the sink. Back and forth she moved without speaking, stacking plates and silverware and glasses, until Boone feared she wasn't going to elaborate on her strange claim at all. When she'd cleared everything she could possibly clear, she steered a hot spray of water into the sink, squirting a healthy serving of dish soap into the steamy cascade. Then, and only then, did she finally acknowledge his request.

"I can't describe it, really," she said over the rush of water. "I just...every year, on my birthday, at some point in the afternoon, for about thirty minutes, I'm almost blindsided by this feeling that there's someone out there thinking about me. Wondering about me. Worrying about me. And all I can figure is that it's my brother, trying to...to...reach me somehow. Does that make sense?"

Strangely, he thought, it did.

She nodded in reply to her own question, then switched the water off and gazed into the mountains of iridescent bubbles.

"It was especially strong today for some reason—like maybe he's moved closer or something somehow."

It took a moment for the impact of her statement to hit Boone. And when it did, it was with the force of a good, solid blow to the back of the head. "Today is your birthday?" he asked.

She nodded, but was still obviously wrapped up in thought. "Yeah. And all afternoon, I've—"

"Today?" he repeated.

She seemed to finally remember that she wasn't alone in the kitchen. When her gaze met his again, it was almost as if she were looking at him for the very first time. "Yeah. Today."

"Lucy…"

"What?"

Boone rose, too, and crossed the kitchen to stand in front of her. "Why didn't you tell me?"

She seemed genuinely confused by his concern. "What difference does it make?"

"What difference…? It's your *birthday*."

"So?"

"So you should be doing something to celebrate."

"Why would I want to celebrate? I just lost everything I own to a fire."

Okay, so she had a point, he thought. Then again, maybe that was all the more reason for her to go out and do something festive—it might take her mind off her recent tragedy.

"But—" he began.

"Besides, I never celebrate my birthday."

"Why not?"

She waved him off and spun back around, then plunged her bare hands into the dishwater, apparently oblivious to the heat signified by the errant coils of steam rising over it. "I just don't," she said.

Boone watched her back grow rigid and had to force himself not to reach over and knead the tension out of her shoulders. "How come?"

"It's just not that important, that's all."

"But..."

"What?" she asked over her shoulder, her voice touched with impatience.

He spun her back around and yanked a dish towel from a hook near the sink, then wiped her hands dry. "*I* should have been cooking *you* dinner tonight, not the other way around. And if you think I'm going to let you do the dishes, you're out of your mind."

"But I'm your slave for a month, remember?"

"You are not now, nor will you ever be my slave."

"But—"

"Lucy, just listen to me for a minute."

Amazingly, to Boone, she snapped her mouth shut and remained silent, but her eyes were nearly electric with anticipation as she pinned him to the spot with her gaze. And for some reason, Boone suddenly forgot whatever it was he had intended to tell her. Instead, all he could do was stand there, wondering what it would be like to engage with her on a regular basis in this kind of verbal byplay and casual touching.

When he realized he was still rubbing the dish towel lightly over her hands to dry them, he tossed it back to the counter and clasped her hands in his, stroking the rough pads of his fingertips lightly across her palm.

Touching her seemed to silence the murmuring tick-tock of the clock overhead, as if time were bestowing upon him a wondrous gift—an opportunity to indulge in Lucy for as long as he wanted to linger there. Her skin was soft and warm beneath his fingers, and she curled her own loosely against his until their hands were almost entwined. Color stained her cheeks, and her lips parted fractionally, as if she wanted to tell him something but couldn't quite get the words out.

Then Boone felt himself spiraling helplessly down into the deep blue beyond of her eyes, and it suddenly occurred to him that he knew how he would answer her earlier question. He knew then that it would be far worse to be alive and have nothing left to want, than to die after living a life rich in the plundering of opportunities. Even if that meant having a regret or two for an opportunity missed.

And he realized, too, that as long as Lucy Dolan walked the earth, he wouldn't have to worry about being alive and having nothing left to want. Which was all the more reason why he knew he should take advantage of this particular opportunity while he could....

Wanting overcame reasoning, action overtook thought, and almost helplessly, he dipped his head and covered her mouth with his. Lucy melted into him immediately, as if she, too, were unable to resist succumbing to whatever strange fire was kindling beneath them. Boone brushed his mouth lightly over hers once, twice, three times, then skimmed a line with his lips, up over her cheek and down along her neck. Sighing a soft sound, she tipped her head back, exposing a creamy expanse of throat to him in invitation, another opportunity he refused to miss.

She smelled of charcoal grill and Ivory soap and all the innocent pleasures life had to offer. She tasted of languid evenings and heady wine and all the things he had forbidden himself to enjoy for too long. Without saying a word, she described an unutterable passion that begged to be savored and spoke promises to fulfill every dream and wish he'd ever embraced. And although he knew no woman was capable of doing that, all Boone could do was fall deeper and deeper and deeper....

The dizzying heat of Boone's mouth on her throat nearly made Lucy collapse. She wasn't sure when the moment had gone from distracted to delirious, only that she couldn't quite recall now what she was supposed to be doing. No matter, she thought vaguely, as a ripple of warm wonder wound through her midsection. Kissing Boone seemed like an enjoyable enough pastime for now.

When he dropped his hands to her waist to pull her closer, she splayed her own hands open over his chest. She reveled in the quick, erratic pulse she felt shuddering beneath her fingertips, marveled at the strength implicit in every rigid muscle she encountered. His neck and jaw were rough with the dark gold stubble of day-old beard, the scratch of the raspy bristles against her sensitive skin creating an oddly enjoyable friction.

He rubbed his cheek against her throat as he nipped her shoulder, and Lucy was helpless to stifle the groan that erupted from some dark, wanting place deep inside her. The ragged sound must have alerted him to her true desire, because he returned his lips to hers and began to consume her more thoroughly. She scored her hands through his hair, noting how the unruly tresses seemed to wind around her fingers as if trying to entrap her, and pulled him closer still.

His mouth on hers was insistent, demanding, needful. And Lucy kissed him back with a command that put his own to shame. Until a swift, piercing stab of pain made her flinch and pull back with a cry.

"Ow!" she exclaimed when he crushed the tender bruise beneath her lip with his. "Ouch, oh…"

Boone jerked backward, hissed an oath under his breath, and spun around until he'd turned his back on her. He braced his hands on his hips so rigidly, she could have traced the swell of each muscle in his forearm with her fingertip had she wanted to. And although she did want to, there was absolutely nothing in his posture that invited such a gesture. On the contrary, he seemed to have shuttered himself into a place that was impenetrable and cold, and in no way accessible with the meager tools she had to work with.

Lucy crossed her arms over her breasts and rubbed her elbows, as if she could ward off the chill of his sudden withdrawal. "Boone?" she ventured quietly.

He tensed even more at the sound of his name, something she would have sworn was impossible. But he offered no other indication that he had heard her at all.

She tried again. "Boone, I—"

"I imagine you probably need to get going."

If his remark hadn't been enough to shut her up, then the miles and miles of icy tundra in his eyes when he reeled back around to face her would have.

"Don't you?" he added.

Although they both knew she had absolutely nowhere to go, Lucy nodded silently. Lifting two fingers to her lips, she whistled for Mack, and after a moment the big tomcat came sauntering into the kitchen, making it halfway across before stopping to stretch long and hard. Then he sat back on his haunches and eyed Boone warily, as if demanding to know just what the hell had been going on.

"I'm sorry," Lucy muttered under her breath. But she said nothing more.

Boone gazed first at the cat, then at Lucy. He watched her withdrawal and acknowledged her distress in the only manner he could at the moment—by trying not to think about it. Later, when he was alone and had his turf back to himself, he could consider what had just happened and try to sort it all out. Later, he could make excuses and tell himself why it could never happen again. Right now, though, he had to make sure Lucy knew there was no more to it than...

What? he wondered. Just what *had* it been about? Later, he told himself again. He'd figure it out later.

"Don't worry about it," he forced himself to say, hoping his voice didn't sound as shaky as the encounter had left him feeling. "It wasn't that big a deal. A birthday kiss, that's all. Just a little, uh...innocent...harmless...birthday kiss. Nothing more than that."

He reined in the hysterical laughter he felt bubbling up at the suggestion that what the two of them had just shared was in any way small.

"A little, um..." he tried again and realized it would be pointless to add anything more. So finally, dismally, he concluded, "Happy, uh...happy birthday, Lucy."

Her eyes had widened at his declaration that what had just transpired was no more significant than the kind of embrace one might receive from an elderly aunt on one's tenth birthday. But she said nothing in response, neither acknowledging his weak, worthless excuse, nor ignoring it. Instead, she only stood there staring at him with those huge, haunted eyes. And with each passing moment, Boone felt like more and more of a heel.

There was so much he felt he should say, but he had no idea how to go about it. How could he discuss what had just happened when he didn't understand it himself? All he'd managed to do was stir up something between the two of them that showed no sign of cooling off anytime soon. So he supposed it was up to him to make sure the fire didn't spread any more than it already had.

He wished he could tell what Lucy was thinking about. Then he was immediately grateful for the fact that he could not. Something told him he didn't want to know what was going on in her head right now. Because he had a feeling her thoughts were just as troubled as his own.

Mack, however, was another story. Boone could easily tell what the cat was thinking about. He formed a perfect isosceles triangle seated there on the floor, but when he caught Boone watching him, he rose and began to wind himself around Lucy's legs. She scooped him up without fanfare and with much affection, and the big cat eyed Boone from the cradle of her arms in a way that said, Don't you wish you were me? Well, you're not. And you never will be.

Don't I know it? Boone responded silently as he gazed back at the animal. Don't I know it?

Without commenting on Boone's assurance that what had just transpired was totally meaningless, Lucy started across the room, throwing one final glance over her shoulder at him before heading for the back door. But all he did was gaze steadily back at her, never moving a muscle.

"Is it okay if I leave the grill and stuff here for now?" she asked softly. "I don't have anywhere to put it, and—"

"That's fine," he interrupted her, his voice as clipped as his words. "Good night, Lucy."

"If you want I could—"

"Good night, Lucy," he repeated emphatically.

She nodded silently, then made her way as quickly and quietly as she could to the back door. She forced herself not to dwell on the kiss that had come out of nowhere and fanned the flames of an already awkward situation. There would be time enough for that later, in the taunting darkness of her motel room, when she was alone. For now, she scooted Mack into his cat carrier on the passenger side of the truck's cab and snapped the seat belt over it.

Then she climbed into the driver's seat and ground the ignition to life, considering Boone's house with an interested eye as she did so. It was an old brick Cape Cod, and as was the case with most old houses, it was beginning to show its age. It looked tired and dissatisfied and in need of some attention. Why, the roof alone was—

Lucy's fingers stilled on her truck keys as an idea unfolded in her brain. It was actually a very good idea, one perfectly suited to her, considering her line of work. And it would go a long way toward repaying Boone the debt she owed him. Because no matter what had just transpired between them in his kitchen a little while ago, she still had that unsettled obligation to take care of.

Satisfaction curled her lips and warmed her belly as she pulled away from his house and made plans. She had to work tomorrow, but the next day was wide open. Everything should work out just fine, she thought.

As long as Boone didn't catch her.

Five

Two mornings after chasing Lucy Dolan from his kitchen, Boone awoke from yet another erotic dream about how that evening *might* have turned out had he not tried to consume her like a vampire. God, what had come over him to do something that stupid? he asked himself through the gauzy haze of half slumber. He wasn't *that* lonely, was he?

Still, when he remembered the way her soft breasts had brushed against his chest, when he recalled the way her fingers had tightened in his hair when he'd tasted her neck, when he thought again about the mix of tenderness and turbulence that seemed to just simmer beneath her surface...

Boone gritted his teeth and expelled a restless sound, then commanded his body to behave itself. It was bad enough waking up this aroused. But to wake up rigid and hear a steady pounding that was way too similar to the rhythm of a man's possession of a woman...

It took a moment for him to realize that the pounding that had awakened him was accompanied by a scraping, and that both sounds were loud. Very loud. And directly above his bedroom ceiling. For a moment, his head still fuzzy from sleep, he could almost convince himself that he was dreaming. Because he couldn't think of a single thing that would cause that kind of scraping and pounding sound. Nothing earthly, anyway. Nothing normal.

Of course, Lucy Dolan was neither of those things, and somehow he knew—he just *knew*—that she was the source of his premature waking, just as she had been so many times over the past few nights. Resigned to his fate, Boone heaved himself out of bed, then scrubbed his hands briskly through his hair. He shrugged on a flannel shirt that he didn't bother to button, cinched up his sweatpants, then stepped into a pair of hiking boots he didn't bother to lace up. With one final sigh, he staggered down the hall toward his front door.

Outside, the brilliant sunlight nearly blinded him, and he grumbled a few bright curses as he knuckled his eyes with loose fists. He was *not* a morning person by any stretch of the imagination, something he recalled with barely controlled hostility as he stumbled down the front steps. Catching himself at the bottom just before he would have barreled headfirst into the bushes, he spun around to look up, fearful even as he did so of what he would see. And although what he saw didn't surprise him in the least, he had to rub his eyes once more and check again, just to be sure he'd seen what he thought he saw.

Yep, he conceded with a frown when he took in the sight for a second time, that's what he thought he saw.

Perched at the edge of his roof, bathed in the pink and yellow glow of early morning, stooped Lucy Dolan. She was dressed once again in those baggy denim overalls that obviously belonged to someone nearly twice her size, an equally large hooded red sweatshirt, tattered work gloves and heavy boots. Her long bangs hung down over her eyes, but she seemed not to notice the impediment, so intent was she on her labor. One by one, she was pulling shingles off of his roof, with a deft efficiency that told Boone she knew exactly what she was doing.

"Lucy," he called out halfheartedly.

But evidently her work was even louder up there than it was down in the yard where he stood, because she didn't bat an eyelash at the summons.

"Lucy," he tried again, a little more loudly.

Yet still she toiled, unheedful of his call.

"Dammit," he muttered under his breath.

Grumbling his discontent, he made his way toward the ladder that she had placed against the end of his house, then scaled it until he could peer over the gutter and onto the roof. He was immediately sorry that he did, because his position afforded him an all-too-nice view of her backside, which, despite the misshapen clothing, was even rounder and curvier than he remembered.

He closed his eyes and pushed the errant thought away. "Lucy!" he shouted again, this time striving to be loud and clear.

She jumped so fast, he was afraid she was going to go tumbling right off the roof. Then she swiftly steadied herself and pivoted around to face him, stooping in that odd, flat-footed way that only children and acrobats seemed capable of achieving. The chill morning air had stained her cheeks and the tip of her nose pink, and her breath emerged from her lips in quick wisps of misty white.

She plopped down on her fanny with an ease that told him she was quite at home on his roof, thank you very much, swiped a sleeve over the perspiration filming her forehead in spite of the cool air, and eyed him levelly. "I didn't know you were home," she said by way of a greeting.

Boone eyed her back. "I kinda figured that."

She had the decency to blush, but not much. "I thought you'd be down at the station. Don't you firefighters work in, like, forty-eight-hour shifts or something?"

He wondered where—and why—she'd done her research on

the matter. "You're half-right. I work a twenty-four-hour shift, then I have forty-eight off."

"Ooooh. I thought it was forty-eight on and forty-eight off."

"So you thought you could sneak this one by me, is that it?"

She nodded shamelessly. "And, by the way, you didn't have to yell," she added tartly. "I heard you the first time."

"Then why didn't you answer me?"

"Because I knew what you were going to say."

"And that would be...?"

She lowered her voice in a terrible imitation of his as she intoned, "Lucy, come down from there this instant."

He smiled in spite of himself. "Uh, yeah, that's pretty close to what I was going to say. Much cleaner without all the profanity I would have thrown in," he added, "but all in all, pretty close."

She smiled back. "See? It wasn't necessary for you to come up here at all."

"Oh, now that's where I think you're wrong," he told her. "Because, Lucy, you *are* going to come down from there this instant."

She shook her head. "Not until I finish for the day."

"Not until you finish what for the day?"

"Putting a new roof on your house."

He stiffened. "I beg your pardon?"

Lucy squinted out at the sun hanging low over the horizon, fiddled with a spatular-looking tool in her hand, then returned her attention to Boone. "I noticed on my way out the other night that, in addition to being an eyesore, your roof probably isn't up to code. What's it been, thirty years since it was replaced?"

"I have no idea," he confessed.

"Well, trust me on this one. You're long overdue."

"Then I'll have a roofer come in and replace it for me."

She smiled brightly. "You already *have* a roofer replacing it for you."

"I do?"

"Yeah. Me. It can go toward working off my enslavement. I won't even charge you for materials." She shrugged. "I know a guy who'll give them to me wholesale."

Boone opened his mouth to comment, realized he had absolutely no idea what to say, so closed it again and stared at her silently.

"I figure I can get this done in a couple of days, three at the most, then I can go to work on whatever else you need done around the house."

"Let me get this straight," Boone said when he finally found his voice again. "You're going to put a new roof on my house."

She smiled brilliantly, tilted her head toward the precarious stack of shingling to her left and nodded. "I thought I made that clear."

"All by yourself," he added.

Again she nodded.

"Um, forgive me for saying so, but that seems like kind of a big undertaking for someone like you."

"Not really," she told him. "I mean, yeah, usually there's three or four of us working on a roof this size, but then we generally get it done in a day. With just me, it'll take a bit longer."

"Won't your boss mind you being away from work?"

She shook her head. "Nah. The season's slowing down a lot. Plus, I've got some personal time coming."

Boone could only watch in curious contemplation the woman seated so comfortably on the eastern slope of his roof, and wonder about her in spite of his own warnings not to. For some reason the occupation she described seemed utterly appropriate for her. Since the moment he'd met her, Lucy hadn't done anything he would have expected, so why should he suddenly think she would hold down an utterly normal, benign job like paralegal or interior decorator? Hell, as far as he was concerned, she could have told him she wrestled alligators for Barnum and Bailey, and he wouldn't have been surprised.

"I see," he finally mumbled in response.

"So get out of my way and let me do my work," she told him when she looked up again.

As if to illustrate her remark, she softly nudged the hand he had flattened against the roof with the toe of her boot. The gesture was a playful one, and Boone couldn't quite stop himself from curling his fingers snugly around her boot. The leather was soft and worn enough that he could detect the subtle swells of her ankle beneath. Before he realized what he was doing, he massaged his fingers over her boot, gradually moving them upward until he was pushing at the denim legs of her overalls.

"Boone..." she said, the sound of his name stirring him from his reverie some.

It was the first time he really took notice of the way she said his name, and he decided immediately that he liked it— all soft and slow and uncertain. Although nothing in that one word indicated she wanted him to stop what he was doing, he somehow managed to halt the progress of his hand at the nether spot where her boot met up with a heavy woolen sock. Before he made contact with her skin. Before he discovered how soft and uncertain she really was.

When he glanced up at her face, she was gazing back at him. Her smile had fallen some, and confusion mingled with agitation in her expression. When he made no move to release her, she tugged lightly to free her foot from his grasp.

"Let go," she said softly.

But for some reason Boone didn't want to let go. So he held tight instead. He wanted to say something about their kiss in the kitchen the other night. He wanted to ask her why it had happened. He wanted her to assure him it would never happen again, then wanted her to assure him that it would. Unfortunately he figured Lucy probably had a couple of questions about that night, too. And frankly, he could no more answer her questions than he could his own.

"Lucy..." he began. But her expression stopped him cold. She gazed back at him, looking earnest and hopeful and worried and desperate. And she looked scared, too, he thought. Boone sighed and wove his fingers anxiously through his sleep-scattered hair. What she looked like was a woman who wanted very badly to forget everything that had happened the other night. She seemed to be silently begging him not to bring it up, please, pretty please, whatever he did, just don't mention it.

"Lucy," he repeated quietly, "come down from there this instant."

Her expression went from grateful to vengeful in seconds. "But—"

"You are *not* going to put a new roof on my house."

"But, Boone—"

"Come down now."

His tone must have convinced her that he wouldn't tolerate any argument on her part. She frowned at him, expelled a disappointed sigh, then made her way toward the edge of the roof where Boone continued to wait for her.

"Aren't you going to bring your tools with you?" he asked.

"I'll get them later," she said noncommittally.

"Maybe you should get them now."

"They'll wait."

Neither moved for several moments, as if each was testing the other's mettle. Finally Boone relented and began to make his way down the ladder. If she thought she was going to come back and finish later, when he wasn't around, she was going to be disappointed. The minute they landed on the ground, he was going inside to consult the Yellow Pages under the listing for Roofers.

When he reached the bottom rung of the ladder, however, he suddenly remembered something and quickly surveyed the grounds. "Wait a minute...where's your cat?" he asked suddenly.

"Mack stayed at the motel today," Lucy said above him. "The lady who runs the place wanted to see if he could do something about the mouse situation in their storage shed."

Boone nodded, but still felt a little wary. "After that, maybe he can do something about the pit bull situation down at the junkyard,'' he muttered under his breath.

"What?"

"Nothing."

Regardless of her assurances to the contrary, he wasn't quite convinced of his safety where that damned cat was concerned. He wouldn't be surprised to find Mack lurking in the bushes, just waiting for Boone to make a wrong move so the malevolent little creature could turn him into one, big, cat treat.

Still wary, Boone hopped to the ground, then stood there to hold the rickety wooden ladder steady while Lucy made her way down. Inevitably his gaze wandered upward to watch her make her descent, and he swallowed hard as he noted the easy, regular sway of her hips every time she dropped down a rung.

How could a woman dressed like a construction worker look that sexy? he wondered. Then he remembered that he hadn't enjoyed much sleep the past few nights, thanks to fires and dreams of Lucy Dolan—which were, in effect, one and the same—and he came to the conclusion that his brain must be addled from exhaustion. Because he could think of no other reason why a woman like her would be wreaking such havoc with his libido.

Without speaking, he motioned her toward the house, and she obediently preceded him into it. Once inside, he hefted the phone book down from its perch atop the refrigerator, and when Lucy peered around his shoulder as he thumbed through the pages, he was assaulted again by the fresh, clean fragrance of her. When the book fell open to the *R*s, Boone slowed his pace, then halted it altogether when he located Roofers.

"Try Magillacuddy Roofing," Lucy suggested. "Don Magillacuddy hired me when all the other outfits thought I couldn't cut it. I owe him."

It was endorsement enough for Boone. He made the call, considered the price range offered to be a workable one, and asked for the free estimate promised by the ad. Then he hung up the phone and turned to face Lucy.

"They said they'd come by this afternoon," he told her.

"And they said it sounded like the job wouldn't take more than a day or two. And they said that this is a slow time for them, so they can probably get to it right away." He rocked back confidently on his heels and tried not to look too satisfied. "And seeing as how you've got some personal time coming," he added, "I guess you won't be the one working on my roof."

She arched her brows in resignation. "Guess not."

His grin was smug.

Lucy scratched her head thoughtfully, then grinned back. "So I guess I'll just have to find some other way to repay you."

His grin fell.

"But that's okay," she added. "I have *lots* more ideas."

Only then did he realize that his adversary was far more wily than he had anticipated. Lucy Dolan, it seemed, was intent on paying him back for saving her cat's life, whether he liked it or not. Hadn't she, after all, *promised* him that?

Boone brightened some at that thought. She had *promised* him, hadn't she? he remembered. Which meant there was no way she was ever going to make good on her debt. Promises were empty, easy bargains to make, because no one—*no one*—ever kept them. They were like communism—nice in theory, but completely unrealistic in practice. In practice, they just never quite lived up to their potential.

Boone had heard a lot of promises in his life, virtually from the day he was born, and none of them had ever become reality. Both of his parents had been alcoholics. And in their brief, irregular sober periods, they had always made promises to their only son.

"We'll go to the ball game Friday," his father would say to him. "Then we'll build that ship in a bottle you bought. And we'll go fishing on Saturday. And we'll spend the whole day together on Sunday, just you and me. I promise you that, Boone. *I promise.*"

His mother, too, had been full of promises during her occasional bouts of coherence. "I'll help you with your home-

work after dinner, sweetheart. Sure, we can go see that movie
you've been wanting to see for so long. Of course you can
join the Boy Scouts. Drum lessons? No problem. *I promise*
you can take drum lessons.''

Then his mother and father would start drinking again and
forget all about the promises they made him. There had been
no ball games or fishing trips. There had been no Scouting or
drum lessons. There had been only promises his parents had
broken, one after another after another.

And then, of course, there had been Genevieve and *her*
promises, he reminded himself relentlessly. Genevieve, the
love of his life. But her promises were still too close to the
surface to think about, so he pushed them resolutely away.
Simply put, Boone had just had his fill of promises. The last
thing he needed or wanted was to be lied to again. Especially
by someone like Lucy Dolan.

He sighed heavily and gazed into her wide, wonderful eyes,
eyes just brimming with hope, candor and an unmistakable
need to be needed. And then he sighed again.

Especially by someone like her.

Men, Lucy thought as she watched Boone slam the tele-
phone book shut, then heave it back to the top of the refrigerator with what seemed to be needless force. Who could understand them? No matter what drove them, regardless of the
kind of life-style that defined them, without noting the envi-
ronment that spawned them, they all had one thing in common: they never made any sense.

Her ex-husband had been the most demanding and least
satisfied man she'd ever known, *and* the least deserving of
special treatment. Yet try to treat him specially she had, day
after day after day. And what had she gotten in return? Booted
out the door and replaced by another woman who was having
even less success pleasing him than she'd had herself.

Hank Dolan had been a man who simply wanted everything,
but who would never have been satisfied with anything. It had

taken Lucy a while to learn that particular lesson, but once mastered, it was one she wasn't likely to forget.

And now she was faced with Boone Cagney, a man who assured her he wanted nothing from her, but who deserved everything she had to give him. A man who refused every meager effort she made to do something nice for him in return for the extraordinary thing he'd done for her. And although Boone was her ex-husband's complete opposite in every other way, he was just as incomprehensible.

Lucy would never, not in a million years, understand the opposite sex.

Okay, so he wasn't going to let her put a new roof on his house, she thought. Fine. There were plenty of other ways to repay him.

She watched him thoughtfully as he opened the freezer and withdrew a can of coffee, then crossed to the other side of the kitchen and began scooping it into his coffeemaker.

"You can have one cup of coffee," he told her over his shoulder. "To warm you up. Then you have to go ho—" He growled in exasperation. "Back to your motel."

She forced a smile as he strode to the freezer, but the gesture was lost on him because he was so valiantly trying to ignore her. "Gee, Boone, you keep sweet talking me like that, you're going to turn my head."

He gritted his teeth at her in something that fell well short of a smile. Then again, she supposed, he probably wasn't trying to smile at her.

"You've interrupted my sleep three times now," he said further. "You're lucky my talk is as sweet as that. I'm not in the best of moods. Don't push me."

"Oh, am I keeping you up?" she asked, feigning innocence. "Well, why didn't you say so? You don't have to stay up on my account. By all means, go back to bed. I'm sure I can find something to do around here to keep me occupied."

He glared at her. "That's what I'm afraid of."

She tried to inject as much sweetness into her voice as she could when she told him, "I won't make a sound, I promise."

"Why not?" he demanded, crossing his arms over his chest in a gesture she could only liken to defensive. "What will you be doing? Waxing my floors? Color coding my CDs? Alphabetizing the contents of my freezer?"

She shrugged. "That's a start."

"Lucy, how many times do I have to say it? I don't want you doing anything for me."

"But—"

"I don't want you to wash my car," he interrupted her objection. "I don't want you to rake my leaves. I don't want you to do my grocery shopping."

"But—"

"I don't want you to bring me breakfast on your way to work, and I don't want you to fix my dinner on your way home."

"But—"

"And I sure as hell don't want you putting a new roof on my house."

"But I have to do *something*."

Once again he drove both hands through his hair in frustration, so forcefully this time that Lucy feared he would be gripping great handfuls of it when he dropped them back to his sides. But his hands were empty when he completed the gesture, opening and closing uselessly in what she could see was impotent, barely controlled, rage.

"Don't you understand?" he finally bit out, obviously straining to remain civil. "Don't you get it?"

She shook her head mutely, still none too certain where his sudden animosity was coming from.

Until he finally cleared it up for her by elaborating—loudly—"I don't want you in my house. I don't want you in my yard. I don't want you underfoot." He paused for only a moment, then said more quietly, more deliberately, "I don't want *you*, Lucy. Period. End of discussion."

It wasn't the sentiment itself that bothered Lucy. Hey, she'd been unwanted all her life, from day one. Her biological parents—her own flesh and blood—hadn't been able to tolerate her beyond eighteen months, and had put her on the open market for whomever might be interested.

Even her adoptive parents—the people who had thought they wanted a child of their own—had changed their minds once they got to know Lucy. She'd grown up hearing her parents vow that if they could have had children of their own, those *real* children would have been *much* different from Lucy, much more to their liking, much more like they were themselves.

Even her ex-husband had tossed her out when she hadn't quite lived up to what he wanted in a woman. Not that that was such a bad thing in the long run, but still... All in all, if the truth be told, Lucy couldn't really remember a time in her life when she *had* been wanted by anyone. So it wasn't really *what* Boone had said that bothered her.

What bothered her was the fact that it was Boone who had said it.

She recalled again the way he had kissed her the other night. Or had she been the one to kiss him? She couldn't quite remember now. From the looks of Boone at the moment, however, Lucy decided the latter must have been the case. Because it had been her birthday, she had been experiencing that odd wistfulness and strange intimacy with a stranger that always overcame her on that date. And clearly, she must have transferred all those feelings onto Boone. Obviously, she must have turned to him with some misplaced need to be needed.

And now he was letting her know exactly how misplaced that need had been.

But instead of responding to his diatribe with an explosion of her own, Lucy only rolled her shoulders, stretched her neck to work out a kink and met his gaze levelly. "That doesn't surprise me," she said softly. "But the fact remains that I have to pay you back. I promised you I would. And I always—"

"I know, I know," he interjected, his voice laced with a weary resolution. "You always pay your debts and you always keep your promises. You'll forgive me if I don't alert the media about that particular development."

Boone sighed heavily, feeling more than a little guilty for his outburst. Lucy didn't deserve the verbal lashing he'd just inflicted upon her, and he still wasn't quite sure where his sudden, shattering anger had come from. Just because he'd been thinking about Genevieve... Well, that didn't give him any right to transfer his bitterness to Lucy. Still, he figured that was probably pretty much what he'd just done.

But, dammit, he was getting sick and tired of her insistence that she was going to pay him back for saving her damned cat. Just what was he going to have to do to get rid of her?

Because he definitely had to get rid of her. There was no question in his mind about that. The more he saw of her, the more she got under his skin. And the more she got under his skin, the harder it was going to be to forget about her when she was gone. Because once this crazy situation was settled—in whatever way—she would be gone. There was no question in his mind about that, either.

She arched her eyebrows in surprise. "You don't sound like you believe me when I tell you that."

"That's because I *don't* believe you," he said. He shifted his attention from Lucy to the coffeemaker, as if watching the slow cascade of the brew would hasten its completion and likewise her departure from his house.

"Are you calling me a liar?" she asked quietly.

Without looking back, he told her, "No. Although there *are* plenty of people out there who do lie when they make promises, knowing full well from the outset that they have no intention of keeping them. I'd say you fall into the other category."

"And what category would that be?"

When he finally turned to look at her again, he saw that although she had behaved coolly while under fire from him, ultimately, she had taken his vitriolic words to heart. Her gaze was level, but her eyes were dark with anguish. Her mouth had flattened into an angry line, but her face was void of any color that might have come with her resentment. Her chin was thrust up at a defiant angle, but her body slumped forward as if she'd been shoved hard from behind while she wasn't looking. And, Boone supposed, in a way she had been.

He sighed heavily again, and this time his words were softer when he spoke. "That would be the category full of people with so-called good intentions who don't *mean* to go back on their word. They just do."

"So then I'm just misguided, is that it?"

He nodded wearily, surprised to find that he was actually sorry to be agreeing with her. "Yeah, that's probably as good a word as any for it. You don't seem like the kind of person who would lie to anyone on purpose, Lucy. But I imagine you've never been able to keep a promise any better than anyone else in the world has."

She glared at him, her eyes lit with challenge. "Oh, yeah?"

He glared back when he saw that she still wasn't going to back down. "Yeah."

"Boy, you sure have a lousy opinion of the human race."

He nodded vigorously. "You're right. I do. I've had enough experience with people to know that they're not the most trustworthy of species."

Lucy shook her head slowly, completely mystified by what Boone had just revealed. "Who did this to you?" she asked him.

"Who did what?" he demanded.

"Who made you so wary? So jaded?"

He laughed, an eerie, joyless sound. "Friends. Family. Fiancée. Take your pick."

Well, that certainly brought her up short. Not so much the fact that he had offered such a wide assortment of loved ones to blame for his bleak outlook, but the fact that one of them apparently was going to be his wife one day. It shouldn't matter to Lucy that Boone was intended for another woman, so why did she care that he had a fiancée? But if the sudden angry tumble of heat in her belly was any indication, she realized she did care. A lot.

Then the phrasing of her thought processes hit her like a Mack truck. *Another woman,* she repeated to herself. Why would she consider his fiancée to be *another* woman, thereby making Lucy the *primary* woman in his life? Lucy wasn't his primary anything. She just barely knew him, for Pete's sake.

"Fiancée?" she repeated, hoping she only imagined the small, achy sound in her voice. "You're engaged?"

He glanced briefly away from her before saying, "Not anymore."

His gesture was quick, his expression full of hurt. It told Lucy everything she needed to know. He still loved the woman to whom he'd been engaged. Whatever had gone wrong, whoever had been responsible for the split, was immaterial. Boone obviously still cared deeply for the woman who had once agreed to be his wife. Just because she wasn't around anymore, that didn't lessen his love for her.

Lucy ignored the little jab of distress that stabbed at her heart and squared her shoulders. "Well, you're wrong about people breaking promises, Boone," she assured him. "At least, you're wrong about me. I do keep my promises. I always have."

He chuckled derisively. "Sure you have."

"You still don't believe me?"

"No."

"Then let me prove it to you."

Boone's head snapped up at her remark, and he realized then how easily Lucy had turned his comments against him. All this time he'd been trying his damnedest to figure out a way to make her see the lunacy of her offer of enslavement, only to wind up setting the stage for his own capitulation. How the hell had that happened?

He sighed again, feeling weary and defeated. "You're not going to go away until you've paid off this nonexistent debt, are you, Lucy?"

She shook her head resolutely, the gesture so fierce and insistent that her dark hair fell down over her eyes. From the looks of her, there was no question that she wanted to put an end to their association as avidly as he did, though whether

her reasons for wanting to have things concluded between them mirrored his own, he had no idea.

He only knew that no matter how hard he fought her, Lucy wasn't going to leave him alone until she'd settled this crazy debt. If he ever hoped to regain any semblance of his former life—or his former sanity, for that matter—he had no choice but to let her have her way.

"All right," he said impatiently, feeling ridiculous as he agreed to her outrageous proposal. "I give up. You can do it, Lucy. You can be my slave for a month. At this point, I'm willing to do whatever it takes to get you out of my life once and for all."

Only when a deep frown pinched her features did he realize he'd spoken the last part of his surrender aloud, and not for the first time since meeting her, he wanted desperately to kick himself in the butt. He hadn't meant to hurt her feelings. He'd just spoken without thinking.

Although, now that he did think about it, Boone reasoned that it might not be such a bad thing to have Lucy misinterpreting his reasons for wanting to be rid of her. Maybe it would be better for them both if she thought his rash words had come about because he didn't like her. It would be infinitely easier than having her know that he *did* like her. A little more than he was comfortable admitting.

He stifled a groan. Just how the hell were they supposed to manage this thing? he wondered. How was he going to last a month, with her creeping a little more under his skin each day, until she took up residence in parts of himself that he really didn't want her visiting?

Then, as he let his gaze rove freely over her face, along the slim column of her neck and the delicate slope of her shoulders, down over the swell of her breasts that even the baggy overalls and sweatshirt couldn't hide... When he remembered the way she had yielded her throat to him that night in the kitchen, and the way her body had gone all soft against his... When he recalled all those lusty, indecent dreams he'd been having the past couple of nights, dreams that featured the two of them tangled up in the most incredible love play... When Boone reconsidered all those things, another question rose with great demand in his brain.

Why was it again that it was so absolutely essential for him to create some distance between them?

Oh, yeah, he remembered. Because it would be suicidal for him to get involved with a woman like her. A woman who was beautiful and warm and charming. A woman who professed to pay debts and keep promises. A woman who was, quite simply, too good to be true. Because a woman like that would no doubt break his heart in a dozen places, starting right here in his kitchen. It would be inevitable.

Genevieve had been too good to be true, too. When Boone first met her, he thought she'd walked right out of his dreams, so perfect had she seemed. She was beautiful, warm, funny and charming. Just like Lucy Dolan. She was exactly what he'd always hoped to find in a lifelong mate. He'd loved her more than he had ever thought it would be possible to love anyone.

And she'd made him promises. Lots of promises. She'd promised to love him forever. She'd promised to be his wife. She'd promised to start a family with him. She'd promised him he would never have to live his life alone again.

For someone like Boone, who had felt alone all his life, and who had grown up having promises continually broken by his parents, Genevieve's pledges had been salve to a wound. Unlike his parents, his ex-fiancée never touched alcohol. Better yet, she never told lies. When she said she was going to do something, she did it.

And when she told Boone she loved him, he believed every word.

Until the day of their wedding, when the whole bridal party showed up at the church on time, except for Genevieve and Conner, Boone's best man. The memory of that afternoon two years ago still made his stomach roil. For nearly five hours—five hours—he had refused to leave the church, assuring the wedding party and what few guests hung around that his blushing bride and his best buddy would be there, they *would*. Genevieve had promised him. She'd *promised*.

Even after everyone else had gone home, even after calling hospitals and the police and everyone else he could think to call, even when he'd been left completely alone in the church with his tuxedo jacket draped over the pew and his black bow tie dangling loose from his collar, he'd still been certain Genevieve would show up. He'd kept waiting for her. And waiting and waiting and waiting.

Then, finally, he'd called home for messages. Even today, Boone had to wonder if the reason he had waited so long to do that was because, subconsciously, he had been afraid of what he would hear. There had been a message on his machine from Genevieve. And according to the dispassionate prerecorded timekeeper, the call was placed precisely eight minutes before the ceremony would have started, had Genevieve and Conner in fact been there.

Almost as if he'd been dreaming, Boone had listened to her soft, delicate, disembodied voice informing him that she and his best man wouldn't be able to make the wedding, because they'd be on their way to Barbados instead. It had been such a cliché, laughable really, he told himself now. Funny, though, how even after two years, he'd never quite managed to find the humor that seemed so obvious in the situation.

In addition to leaving him at the altar, Genevieve had left him financially strapped. She'd kept the engagement ring Boone had been in no position to afford in the first place— and hadn't yet paid off—and she'd hocked it for half the cash it had cost him to buy it. She'd also left him holding the bag on a mortgage loan he hadn't been able to pay on his salary alone, something that had taken him months to undo and nearly wrecked his credit rating. Then she and his best buddy—his best man—had enjoyed the prepaid Caribbean cruise that was supposed to have been his honeymoon.

Genevieve had taken him to the cleaners, both financially and emotionally. After what she had done to him, Boone had promised himself he would never, not in a million years, not if she were the last female on the planet, allow himself to get involved with a woman who seemed too good to be true. And Lucy Dolan was exactly that.

But then, he taunted himself, hadn't he always said no one ever kept their promises? Didn't that include promises people made to themselves?

Of course not, he countered himself immediately. Promises you made to yourself were the only ones that *could* be kept. You just had to work really, really hard at it. And he vowed then and there to do just that. He *promised* himself that he would.

Boone tried to reassure himself that it wouldn't take a month for Lucy to complete her task. Regardless of her promise that she would be his slave for that length of time, he knew she'd never keep her word. A week at the outside. That's how long he gauged it would be before she tired of her game and called it quits, satisfied that she'd done enough to even the score between them. If he could just stand her hanging around for seven days, he told himself, he'd be in the clear once and for all.

"When do you want to start?" he asked her wearily.

She shrugged, but the gesture was in no way casual. "No time like the present, right?"

Boone started to nod, but stopped himself. "How about Friday instead?" he asked, citing a time two days hence.

It would be better, he decided, to have her start her enslavement while he was working a shift at the station. A guarantee of twenty-four hours without Lucy underfoot seemed like a very good idea at the moment, even if there was a good chance that part of that twenty-four hours could be potentially life threatening. It wasn't like he was out of danger at home. Not for the next thirty days anyway.

"That'll give you a little time to enjoy your last few days of freedom," he told her. "Go back to your motel and get some rest, Lucy. If you're going to be a slave for thirty days, you're going to need it."

She opened her mouth to protest, but something in his expression must have made her think twice about objecting. Instead, she nodded, and he was surprised that she didn't put up a fight about staying to wash his car or bake him some cookies or balance his checkbook. Instead, she just murmured something about collecting her tools and ladder on the way out, then turned silently and made her way through the kitchen door.

And as the front door creaked shut behind her, all Boone could do was marvel at his disappointment that for once, Lucy had done exactly what he'd told her to do.

Evidently, he thought, wondering why the realization should send such a warm thrill buzzing through his system, she was *really* going to take this whole slave business to heart.

Six

***

"But you said you liked this color."

Lucy stood in the middle of Boone's spare bedroom holding a still-damp paint roller in one hand and a selection of paint chips in the other. Beneath her feet was one of many huge, paint-spattered tarpaulins that she had tossed over the floor and all the furnishings. But truth be told, Boone was hard-pressed to identify just where the tarps ended and Lucy began.

She had tied a threadbare bandanna, dotted with scores of shades of paint, pirate-style over her hair, and her T-shirt, which had once probably been white, was splashed with dozens more colors ranging from pastel yellow to electric blue. The baggy denim overalls she normally wore had been replaced by a pair of baggy, paint-smeared, painter's overalls, and she looked very apprehensive.

Boone couldn't blame her. The color she'd just finished rolling onto the walls in his spare bedroom made him feel more than a little uneasy, too. It was bad enough that he'd let her talk him into painting the entire house. Now she had to go and paint it—

"Pink," he muttered distastefully. "I never said I liked pink."

"It's not pink," she countered. "It's terra-cotta."

He eyed the color on the walls surrounding him on all four sides and frowned. "No, that's pink."

"It's terra-cotta," she insisted, holding up the booklet of paint chips. "Look. It says so right here."

Boone eyed the paint sample warily. He'd barely taken the time to note it yesterday morning, when Lucy had reported for her first day of slavery. At the time he'd been late for work and in a big hurry to leave the house. When she'd told him she thought some of his rooms could use brightening—"Let's face it, that icky eggshell throughout the entire house just *has* to go"—and that she wanted to do a little painting, he'd told her she was out of her mind, that the color was just fine, thanks, and why didn't she take the day off and go home?

But, of course, she had taken exception to his suggestion and, as always, she'd argued with him. For five full minutes, they'd both spoken nonstop, neither paying any heed to what the other was saying.

Then Boone had remembered it was impossible to change Lucy's mind. So, in a last-ditch effort to be on time for his shift, he'd agreed to let her paint his house. The activity had seemed like something harmless enough to keep her occupied and out of his hair. And when she'd fanned a few sample chips out for his approval, he'd scanned them quickly and told her they were fine. Of course, at the time he hadn't really been paying attention, and he hadn't realized one of those colors was—

"Pink. That's definitely pink," he repeated.

"Will you just look at this paint chip again," Lucy demanded, waving it under his nose. "What does that say, right there under that color?"

Boone smiled triumphantly. "It says Desert Sunset."

She nodded. "Right. Desert Sunset."

"It does *not* say Terra-Cotta."

She threw him a look that indicated she thought he was just this side of complete lunacy. "Well, what do you think a desert sunset is?"

"It's pink, if this color is any indication."

"It's *not* pink," she insisted. "It's orange. And this color—" She pointed to the paint chip in her hand again. "This color is too orangey to be pink. It's terra-cotta."

Giving her the benefit of the doubt, Boone studied the four walls again. He'd run some errands after leaving the station that morning, then he'd returned home to be assaulted by the acrid smell of paint accompanying Lucy's off-key belting out of "Blues in the Night." As he'd stood with his front door ajar behind him to listen for a few minutes, he realized she was altering every verse into some new color, singing out "Reds in the Night" or "Mauves in the Night" or "Pinks in the Night."

That should have been his first clue that he wasn't going to like what he saw.

When he'd followed her husky voice back to his spare room, he'd found her still singing, shimmying down a ladder as if she were a burlesque queen. Her heart-shaped fanny had been lovingly molded by her painter's pants and kissed with patches of color in places Boone found himself wanting to reach out and touch. The color in question happened to be pink.

That should have been his second clue.

But Boone had been too focused on the way she was dancing down the ladder to pay much attention to what she'd done to his walls. Instead, suddenly, he'd decided that maybe Lucy was right. Maybe his house did need a good painting. He hadn't done any himself since he'd moved in nearly two years ago, and some of the rooms did have a rather dingy appearance. Of course, that was before he realized she was going to paint the place—

"Pink. It's pink," he repeated. "And I won't have pink in my house."

She folded her arms resolutely over her midsection. "Well, I'm not painting it again."

"Oh, yes, you are."

"Just wait till it dries," she entreated. "And let me put on a second coat. Paint never takes on its true color until it's dry and has a second coat. After that, if you still think it's pink, then *maybe* I'll paint over it."

"*Maybe* you'll paint over it?" he repeated. "I thought you were my slave. I thought you were going to do whatever I told you to do."

"Well, within reason," she said.

He gaped at her. "Oh, sure, *now* you add that convenient little disclaimer."

Lucy gaped back. "Well, surely you didn't think I would enslave myself to a man I hardly know without a disclaimer. Just what kind of woman do you think I am?"

Boone had had just about all he was going to take. With an exasperated growl, he spun around and left the room, rubbing his temples to ward off a throbbing headache that wasn't entirely caused by paint fumes. He was barely one day into his month-long agreement with Lucy, and already he could feel himself about to explode. With frustration, with animosity, with helplessness, with exhaustion, with...

Desire. Dammit, that was what was really causing him to feel so outraged right now...and whenever he found himself within fifty feet of Lucy. In spite of her painter's garb and the fact that she'd just painted part of his house pink—*pink*, for God's sake—all Boone could think about was how much he wanted to pull her close, lose himself in her warmth and laughter and wipe those paint smears off the seat of her pants. No other woman could possibly look good dressed the way she was dressed right now. But Lucy Dolan somehow managed to make paint stains look sexy.

It made no sense. She was in no way like the women he normally dated these days. These days Boone only allowed himself to be attracted to women he could peg nicely and narrowly into a neat little type. And that type was *predictable*.

The only kind of women he involved himself with—and only on a superficial level at that—were the kind of women he could sum up quickly and categorize with fairly little effort.

He liked women whose behavior he could gauge from the moment he met them. Women who offered no surprises. Boone had resolved a long time ago that the women he dated would be, above all else, free of expectation.

Of course, that meant the women he dated were generally rather boring and not much fun to be around, but then a man had to make concessions if he wanted to make sure he was never double-crossed again.

And now Lucy Dolan had come along and defied that resolution. She was kooky, she was candid, she was spontaneous, and she treated her cat as if the animal were a long-lost sibling. Above all, she was unpredictable. The kind of woman who would easily say one thing and do another. A woman who would doubtless never keep her word.

And if Boone let her get too close, she would crush him under her thumb exactly as Genevieve had done.

"Boone, wait. I need to ask you something."

He kept walking down the hall toward the stairs that led to his bedroom, telling himself that maybe if he ignored Lucy, she would just go away. "What is it? I have things I need to do."

He didn't stop walking until he scaled the stairs two at a time and stood before his closet door, which he swung open with considerably more force than was necessary before inspecting the contents, pretending he knew what he was looking for.

"Boo-oo-oone," he heard Lucy complain, the distance of her voice indicating she was still climbing the stairs.

"What?" he snapped.

"I need to ask you something important."

This time her voice was much closer—right behind him, in fact, something he discovered the hard way when he whirled around and spun right into her, grabbing her by the waist before she could go stumbling backward. In response, Lucy au-

tomatically tried to steady herself by grasping his upper arms
with considerable force. When she did, the paint chips she'd
been holding went tumbling to the floor between them, completely unnoticed.

For a long time neither of them moved. They only stood
holding on to each other as if neither wanted to be the first to
alter the position. Boone gazed down at Lucy, noting a small
spatter of Desert Sunset that had stained her face right above
her lip. Without realizing what he was doing, he removed one
hand from her waist to stroke his thumb over the pink—yes,
it was definitely pink—smudge, in a manner that was far too
gentle to erase it. And when she touched her tongue lightly to
the corner of her mouth where his fingertip lingered, his stomach clutched convulsively into a knot.

When he felt like he was able to speak without having his
voice crack with an embarrassing squeak, he cleared his throat
raggedly and asked, "What do you want, Lucy?"

He forced himself to inject an impatience he didn't necessarily feel—not for her, anyway—into his voice in an effort
to preserve the physical and emotional distance he was striving
so hard to maintain. But when he saw the way she continued
to look at him, her eyes brimming with something warm and
wistful and wanton, he started to forget again why it was so
essential that he keep her at a literal and figurative arm's
length.

There was no way he was going to be able to survive a
month of having her in his house. Or even a week, for that
matter, he thought, reminding himself again of the certainty
that Lucy would go back on her word in no time at all. He
was far too attracted to her already, and seeing her on a daily
basis would only compound his desire to have her.

She kept staring at him for a moment in silence, as if she
couldn't recall exactly what she was doing in his bedroom or
what she had wanted to ask him. Then she suddenly snapped
out of her reverie, her eyes widening in something he could
only liken to panic. She, too, took several steps backward, and

with a jerky motion, bent to scoop up the booklet of paint chips that she had dropped.

"Um..." she began as she sorted quickly through the spiral bound cards, "hang on a second...let me see here..."

When she finally found what she was looking for and glanced up from the paint selection again, her smile was winsome and hopeful, and Boone discovered uncomfortably that Lucy's influence over his body seemed to be growing by leaps and bounds. Unfortunately, shifting his weight to his other foot only compounded his discomfort. He bit back a groan and hoped she wouldn't notice his condition.

"What, um..." she began again. She indicated a color on one card that was a rather unsuccessful cross between blue and green that somehow managed to look a little gray. "What do you think of this color for your bedroom?" she asked.

Boone sighed heavily. "Just how late are you planning to stay today?"

She scrunched up her shoulders and let them drop again. "I don't know. No offense, but there's a lot that needs to be done around here."

"And you have a month to do it," he pointed out.

She shrugged again, this time dropping her gaze back down at the paint chips. "I'm not sure I can finish everything I need to get done in thirty days."

"Just how much more are you planning to do?"

"I don't know," she said again vaguely, her voice growing smaller with every word she spoke. "I just thought maybe you could use the extra help."

Boone nodded, even though he knew she wouldn't see the gesture, staring down at the floor the way she was. He was gradually beginning to understand that maybe Lucy was doing this as much for herself as she was for him. Whether she realized it or not, she seemed to need to be needed by someone. And maybe the only way she could do that was by forcing herself into someone's life the way she had barged into his.

"That color's okay," he said quietly, not sure why he suddenly felt so cooperative. "But I think a straight blue would be better."

When she glanced up at him again, he could swear her expression was grateful. Terrific, he thought. Just the reaction he'd always hoped to inspire in a woman—gratitude.

She flipped through the selection of colors again, stopping on a card that offered an assortment of blues and purples. "How about this one?" she asked, pointing to a medium blue that Boone decided was actually kind of nice.

"I like that one," he told her.

"That's Ocean Mist," she informed him.

He nodded agreeably. "Sounds soothing." Which was exactly what he needed right now.

"Okay, Ocean Mist in the bedroom it is." Her sad smile brightened some as she added, "And just wait till you see what I have in store for the living room. You won't recognize this place when I'm finished with it."

Boone pinched the bridge of his nose between his thumb and forefinger in an effort to ward off a headache he felt threatening. "That's what I'm afraid of, Lucy," he muttered quietly. "That's what I'm afraid of."

For the next two weeks, Lucy was the best little slave she could possibly be. As she'd told Boone, when the weather turned cooler, construction work tended to slow, and she took advantage of the three weeks' worth of vacation and personal time she hadn't yet used, time she had planned on enjoying over the holidays, had it not been for her enslavement.

But hey, she'd reasoned, what was the point of taking time off at the holidays when one would doubtless wind up spending one's days with one's cat at a budget level motor inn, celebrating little more than the fact that, thanks to cable, one could view *It's a Wonderful Life* on fifty-seven channels?

Her employer had understood perfectly her request for time off, considering the loss of her house and so much more, and Lucy hadn't corrected his assumption. Of course she did use some of the time personally—fruitlessly surveying houses on the market in the hopes of finding one to her liking, buying clothes and other items that were essential for basic survival— but the bulk of her time went to Boone. Or, more specifically, to Boone's house. Because, frankly, Lucy didn't see too much of the man himself.

When he wasn't working, he always seemed to have something else very pressing to attend to. She got the not-so-subtle impression, though, that his frequent jaunts were so...well, frequent...because he just wanted to be someplace where Lucy wasn't. His activities varied from poker with the boys to a movie by himself to a hot date with some unspecified redhead whose numerous attributes he praised profusely.

Seemingly within moments of Lucy's arrival at his house every day, he was headed out the door to somewhere else. He even gave her a key to the front door—a gesture she considered entirely unprecipitated—so that she could come and go at will during his shifts and to limit his need for even that small exchange of conversation.

Without Boone underfoot, Lucy was quick to tend to all the little things around his house that needed fixing or improving. When she finished painting the interior, she went to work on correcting his appalling lack of domestic organization.

She cleaned out his refrigerator—wrinkling her nose in disgust at some of the things she found there, things that couldn't possibly have been organic at any point in time—and she restocked it with groceries that were much healthier, heartier and tastier, as far as she was concerned. She rearranged his cabinets so that they made considerably more sense—to her, at least—and she had someone come in to slipcover his living room furniture with fabrics she thought were infinitely more appealing than the drab beiges and browns he had chosen himself. Then, deciding he hadn't made nearly as effective a use of space as he could have, she rearranged the furniture to create a much more homey atmosphere.

She even found herself wishing it weren't autumn, normally her favorite season, so that she could set out some pansies and marigolds along the front walk and plant a dogwood tree in a bare spot in the backyard to provide some wonderful color and shade in the years to come. Maybe she could stop by in the spring to do a little landscaping, she thought. Surely Boone wouldn't mind. In the meantime, she satisfied her green thumb by planting an herb garden in a collection of terra cotta pots she placed on the window ledge above the kitchen sink.

While she did all these things for Boone, she was almost always alone. Happily alone. Happily, gloriously alone. Alone, alone, alone. Yep, just the way she wanted to be. No Boone Cagney in sight. No one to bother her. No one to argue with her. No one to counter every move she made. Exactly the way she liked it. Yes, sirree. Because with Boone so conveniently out of the way, she scarcely thought about him at all.

Most of the time, anyway. Oh, there were those occasions when she found her mind drifting from the task at hand, and invariably Boone's image would creep up from the dark recesses of her brain and embed itself firmly in her reveries, often to the point where she just couldn't shake him off no matter how hard she tried.

And, okay, sometimes he would be shirtless in those reveries. And a couple of times this dream version of Boone would take her in his arms and engage her in the most erotic visions of foreplay she had ever been able to imagine.

All right, and truth be told, one time they made love in her daydreams. But only once. After that, she made herself call a halt to her fantasies before they had a chance to go too far, because that one imaginary time with Boone was more than enough to remind her of what she was missing in reality. And even though she was mature enough to admit that the world didn't revolve around sex, the fact that sex had been completely removed from her own personal world for the past few years made Lucy wonder what was the big deal about the world revolving, anyway.

"Hey, who needs to see another day dawn?" she asked Mack on just such an occasion precisely two weeks into her self-imposed slavery.

The two of them were in Boone's basement doing the laundry, Lucy standing before the washer, snapping his clothes fiercely as she removed each piece, Mack curled up in the shape of a meat loaf atop the gently whirring dryer, his eyes closed in barely controlled ecstasy, his purr rumbling twice as loudly as the big machine's.

Lucy couldn't help but smile, remembering how he'd always loved lying on top of the warm, softly vibrating dryer at home. The one that had burned her house to the ground. Not for the first time since that night, she forced down a feeling of melancholy at all that she had lost, and reminded herself that she still had the most important things in life.

Well, most of them, anyway.

"I mean, what's the point of waking up every morning," she mused, uncaring of whether Mack paid her any mind or not, "if all I'm going to do is move mechanically through the day without much notice of anything and then go to bed at night feeling completely unchanged? Who needs it?"

Normally Lucy wasn't such a whiner. Normally she scarcely took much notice of the way she spent her days—or her nights. Which was probably why she moved through them so mechanically. Of course, that was back before she had been spending her days with Boone. Or, rather, with Boone's house. Now *mechanical* was the last thing she felt.

Because Boone had been home occasionally. The two of them had even shared a few meals together. And they'd had a number of conversations, some of which had actually lasted longer than five minutes and hadn't wound up with their voices raised. Lucy had forgotten how much fun it could be to spend time with another human being. Certainly she loved having Mack as her main companion in life, but even she had to concede that he was a bit lacking in the area of conversation. Oh, sure, he could get his point across when he needed to, but his vocabulary was just a smidgen limited.

Boone, on the other hand, had proved to be a very energetic conversationalist. Of course, he was usually telling her she couldn't do something she wanted to do where his house or the improvement of his life-style was concerned, but at least his language was colorful. Sometimes a little *too* colorful, like when he came home to find that she had cleaned out his attic and donated all of his *National Geographic* magazines predating World War II to a local high school, but still...

Her foul mood today was simply a result of the fact that she was so tired, she told herself now. Slavery was more exhausting than she'd realized it would be. Even with Boone insisting every time she showed up at his front door that there was nothing for her to do and why didn't she just take the day off, she always found something undone.

Like an overflowing laundry hamper, she thought now, reaching back into the washer to withdraw the last item inside. She felt warmth creep into her cheeks when she pulled that item out and recognized it for what it was—a pair of men's briefs.

It was just underwear, she reminded herself, fingering the damp fabric as if it were an expensive silk garment in danger of dissolving. She'd done her ex-husband's laundry for almost five years, and never once had she paid the slightest bit of attention to his underthings. So how come a pair of plain, white cotton briefs, undecorated save the word *Jockey* embroidered around the waistband, suddenly caused her heart to race wildly behind her rib cage?

"Because you're a doofus," she answered herself aloud.

When Mack opened one eye and considered her thoughtfully, Lucy snapped her mouth shut again and berated herself in silence. Because you're entirely too moved by things you have no business being moved by. Like Boone Cagney's underwear. And, even more problematic, like Boone Cagney.

As if summoned by her thoughts, she heard the front door slam closed upstairs and knew he was home from work. She glanced down at her watch. Not even eleven-fifteen. He was early. He must have run out of the superficial errands he normally attended to after a shift to keep him busy and out of her presence.

She went back to sorting through the damp laundry she'd removed from the machine as she listened to his heavy tread and the squeak of the hardwood floors above her. She knew what was coming next. It was the same thing that happened every time Boone returned home after a twenty-four-hour shift at the station, the bulk of which time *she'd* spent slaving away. His methodical pace down the hall was followed by a quick, steady thump-thump-thump-thump-thump as he climbed the stairs to his bedroom.

Lucy paused in her sorting, rolling her eyes toward the basement ceiling, and waited. Five, four, three, two, one...

"Lucy!"

The bellow of her name fairly shook the house at its foundations. She squeezed her eyes shut, waiting for the rest of the explosion that inevitably followed.

"What the hell have you done!"

She sighed and opened her eyes. As always, she hadn't done anything. Just cleaned up a little. Just rearranged things a little. Just completely redecorated his bedroom a little.

At the roar of Boone's voice, Mack had leapt down from the dryer and started to pace, his tail expanding to the size of a Louisville Slugger. Lucy adopted her most reassuring voice as she said, "It's okay, sweetie. Mr. Cagney's just tired after his shift at work. Don't you worry about a thing."

"Lucy!" he bellowed again, bringing forth a low, level growl from Mack. "Come upstairs this instant!"

She sighed impatiently. Men. So demanding.

"You wait here," she told the cat. "I'll take care of this."

Mack eyed her suspiciously, then leapt back up to the dryer and curled himself into a restive ball. "Rowr," he said in his rusty meow. And for some reason, Lucy interpreted the comment to mean, "Be careful."

She hastily emptied and refilled the dryer before accommodating Boone's request, then gathered the laundry basket full of clean clothes and took her time wending her way up to his bedroom. When she topped the last step, she saw him, standing with his back to her at the foot of the bed, still dressed in his firefighter's uniform, his hands on his hips, his back ramrod straight.

"Hi, Boone," she greeted him, as brightly as she could. "How was your shift?"

He didn't turn around, but she could tell that his breathing was barely controlled when he replied, "I was nearly killed in a flashover."

Her breath caught in her throat. "You what?"

"But that was nothing compared to the near-fatal heart attack I just had when I came into my bedroom."

She smiled a little tenuously. "You don't have to thank me. It was my pleasure."

He spun around and glared at her menacingly. "Th-thank you?" he sputtered, throwing his arms out to his sides. "*Thank you?* For this? Just what the hell have you done?" He jabbed a thumb over his shoulder. "What is that *thing* on my bed?"

She gazed past him at the queen-sized bed, swallowing with some difficulty. "It's...it's a...a new bedspread," she told him, the tremor in her voice mirroring the tremble that shook her body. "What? You don't like it?"

If possible, his entire body went even more rigid. "What do you think?"

"But the old one was threadbare. Not to mention ugly. I mean, Boone, come on... That macho plaid stuff went out with the seventies."

"So you replaced it with *that?*"

"What's wrong with that? It's very Martha Stewart. Very happening. Very now."

"What it is is very...very..."

Uh-oh. He was at a loss for words, Lucy thought. That wasn't a good sign at all. Normally Boone had more than enough words to express his outrage. Most of them weren't exactly socially acceptable, but there were always a lot of them.

He spun around and looked at the bed again. "What are those things in the pattern, anyway?"

She tried to smile, but the gesture fell short. "They,

um...they're violets. Nice, huh? Don't they go beautifully with the Ocean Mist?''

He pivoted around to face her again, but said nothing, the heated anger in his eyes starting to smolder. Uh-oh.

"Actually,'' she tried again, hoping to appease him some, "I couldn't decide between that one and the one with the—'' she cleared her throat indelicately "—the, uh, fruit baskets.''

"Fruit baskets,'' he repeated dispassionately.

She nodded. "Uh-huh. But I...I chose the one with the violets because it seemed...more...masculine.'' Her voice trailed off when the smoldering anger in his eyes spontaneously combusted.

"Masculine?'' he asked, his voice too quiet for her comfort. He thrust his thumb backward again, but didn't turn around. "You call that thing masculine?''

She nodded weakly. "Yeah, it doesn't have a ruffle like the other one did.''

He glared at her harder.

"Look,'' she tried again, in spite of the fact that any explanation she offered at this point was going to be lame at best. "All I've tried to do is make a few improvements around your house. If you don't like them—''

"*My* house?'' he interrupted her. "This isn't *my* house. It's your house. Nothing here is anything like it was when it was *my* house.''

Lucy bit her lip and gazed at him mutely and wished he would stop glaring at her like that.

Boone clapped a hand over his face, hoping somehow to block his vision entirely of the thing on his bed and the woman who had put it there. Unfortunately even his big hand couldn't quite hide all the things she had done to his room. *His* room. He dropped his hand to his side and reluctantly took in the scene again.

In addition to the new bedspread, Lucy had hung new curtains on the two dormer windows, curtains that inevitably boasted the same pattern as the bedspread. She'd removed the rag rug he'd bought at a yard sale ten years ago and replaced it with one of those hooked, flowery ones that were so prevalent in the Spiegel catalogue. Potted plants lined the window seats that had earlier played host to about two years' worth of *Firehouse* magazine and a stack of Stephen Coonts novels. Small pen-and-ink drawings of herbs hung on the wall where once had been posted Boone's most prized possession in the world—a boar's head clutching a cigar in its bared teeth, a battered Stetson settled atop its head.

He wished he could be angrier at Lucy. Unfortunately he was way too angry with himself to have any left over for her.

How had he let things go this far? he demanded of himself. Two weeks of her indenture had passed and she was still underfoot, as intrusive as ever. He'd had no idea such a small woman would have such a catastrophic effect on his life. Just how long was it going to take her to go back on her word? How much longer was he going to have to put up with her invasion before she broke her promise? This insistence of hers to make good on her vow was really getting him steamed.

He turned to look at Lucy again, noting that she still clutched a basket full of his laundry under one arm, as if she'd been too scared to move since topping the last step. Her cheeks were flushed with pink, her eyes were dark and guarded, her lips were parted fractionally, as if she needed a bit more air. She was dressed as masculinely as usual in blue jeans, a flannel shirt and hiking boots, and as always, she somehow made the butch apparel seem sexy as hell.

And suddenly, Boone thought of something that just might hasten her departure from his life.

"Lucy?" he asked, making a supreme effort to keep his voice level, steady, harmless.

She swallowed hard, but otherwise remained motionless. "Yes, Boone?"

"Why are you doing all this?"

"I told you—I owe you. Big."

He nodded. "That's right. You do. And you know…I think it's about time you paid up. In full."

Seven

The color in Lucy's face deepened as her body went stiff, and Boone could see that she was surprised by—and a little uneasy about—his sudden and complete turnabout in opinion.

"You owe me your life, don't you?" he asked.

She nodded in response, but said nothing.

"And you owe me Mack's life, too."

Another silent nod.

"As you yourself said, the debt you have to repay is huge. Isn't that what you said, Lucy?"

"Yes." The one-word response was hoarse and barely perceptible.

"So huge," Boone continued quietly, carefully, "that the only way you could think to repay it was to offer yourself as my slave for one month. As my *slave*, Lucy. That's what you *promised*, isn't it?"

"Yes." If possible, her voice was even softer when she replied that time. But she still said nothing more than that.

"And considering the fact that I basically own you—however temporarily—so far I've asked very little of you, haven't I?''

"Yes."

"In fact, so far, I've *asked* for nothing from you. You've done everything on your own. Isn't that true, Lucy?''

"Yes."

He hesitated, his gaze never leaving hers. He settled his hands on his hips and shifted his weight to one foot. "It's good that you've gotten so used to the word *yes*," he told her, injecting what he hoped was just the right amount of menace in his voice. "Because suddenly there *is* something I want you to do. And you have to do it, you have to say 'yes,' because you're my slave, aren't you?''

Her only response was to meet his gaze levelly and without comment. She knew what was coming, he thought. It was abundantly clear that she knew what he was going to ask her— no, what he was going to *command* her—to do. He could tell by the glitter of invitation in her eyes and the challenging tilt of her chin. What she didn't know was just how serious he was about issuing the command. Nor did she know how far he was willing to carry it. And it was going to be interesting— not to mention *his pleasure*—to find out how far she was willing to go herself.

"Put down the basket, Lucy."

Without hesitation, she bent to set the laundry on the floor.

"Come here."

This time she did hesitate.

"Now."

At the one-word order, she inched forward, seeming to take forever to close the scant three feet of distance that separated them. When she stood before Boone, she stared straight ahead, at the buttons of his shirt instead of his face. Her black hair glistened almost blue in the sunlight streaming through the windows, and she smelled of linens warmed by a summer day. And as much as he told himself he was only doing what he was about to do because he wanted to scare her off once and for all, he knew it was really because he just wanted Lucy.

Wanted her more than he'd ever wanted anything in his life.

"Look at me," he said softly.

When she tilted her head back to meet his gaze, the blue of her eyes was nearly eclipsed by the wide expansion of her pupils. Her ivory skin was dusted faintly with pink, her full mouth ripe and red and whisper soft.

"Kiss me," he instructed her.

Her lips parted just a breath, as if she were about to object, but she said nothing. Instead she curled her fingers gingerly around his nape, tipped her head to the side, rose up on tiptoe, closed her eyes...and covered his mouth with hers. Her kiss was tentative, gentle, tender. It was the kiss of a first-time lover. And it made Boone hungry for more.

But just as he was about to join in, Lucy stepped back and dropped her hand to her side again. Her chest rose and fell raggedly, as if she couldn't quite control her breathing, and her pulse danced wildly at the base of her throat.

"There," she whispered roughly. "I kissed you. That ought to take care of it."

"Not quite."

Her eyes widened again, growing even darker.

Boone inhaled deeply, held the breath in his chest for a moment, then released it in a slow, steady stream. "Unbutton your shirt," he said.

"Wh—"

"Unbutton your shirt, Lucy."

"But—"

"You're my slave, aren't you? Do it."

She met his gaze levelly, narrowing her eyes in what he couldn't decide was suspicion or challenge. Then, much to his surprise and delight, she lifted her hand to the top button of her shirt and slipped it through its hole. Then she dropped her hand to the next button and unfastened it, too. Then the next, and the next, and the next. Without him having to ask, she jerked her shirttail free of her jeans and loosed the remaining bindings. Then she dropped her hands to her sides again, and stood before him thoroughly unbuttoned.

Boone's breath had caught in his throat somewhere around button number three. Because although Lucy may have dressed like a construction worker on the outside, beneath all the flannel and denim lay the promise of lingerie paradise. A murmur of raspberry-colored lace peeked out from between the folds of her shirt, the hue only a few shades off from the deep flush creeping up from between breasts even fuller than he'd anticipated.

"More," he said helplessly, voicing his thoughts out loud. His gaze traveled back up to fasten with hers. "I want to see more."

With only a minor hesitation this time, Lucy caught the sides of her shirt and opened it wide, her eyes penetrating his as she completed the action.

"Take it off," he told her.

She shrugged out of the garment completely and tossed it to the floor, and Boone felt himself ripening fast. Her nipples puckered under the translucent lace, and her breasts strained against the delicate fabric as if aching to be freed.

"Now the jeans," he said, hoping he only imagined the coarseness in his voice.

"What about the jeans?" she asked, her own voice bearing no resemblance to the light, almost musical timbre he'd become accustomed to hearing from her. Now Lucy's voice was low and husky, as if she were experiencing the same kind of arousal Boone was feeling himself.

"Take them off," he told her. "Now."

Again, with little hesitation, Lucy moved her hands to the button on her fly and opened it. Slowly, oh, God, so slowly, she lowered the zipper, until a bikini panty of the same lace as her brassiere was visible. She moved to sit on his bed long enough to slip off her hiking boots and socks, then stood again and gripped the waistband of her jeans. Again, her gaze never faltering from his, Lucy skimmed the softly worn denim down the length of her legs until they were nothing but a pool of faded blue around her ankles. Then she stepped out of them and kicked them away.

She stood straight and proud before him, eyes defiant, one dark eyebrow arched in challenge. Her chest rose and fell rapidly with her ragged respiration, her ivory skin flushing from the base of her throat to her concave belly. He could see that she was a little frightened—possibly even as frightened as he was himself—of what was happening. But she seemed no more willing to stop it from coming than he was.

Evidently, Boone thought, she was willing to go farther than he'd planned on her going. Instead of him scaring her off, she was daring him to come on. He felt himself tighten even more, his entire body now rigid with wanting her. And he understood then that she was his for the taking.

She was his slave. And he wanted to own her. Body, mind and soul. It was only fair, after all, he reasoned. Because after this, he knew she would always possess him completely.

"Now then," he managed to get out. "Come here and kiss me again. Properly this time."

Lucy swallowed hard and tried to quiet the runaway racing of her heart. God help her, she had never been more aroused in her life. Her entire body hummed with anticipation and need and desire. A fire crackled just beneath the surface of her skin that threatened to explode the instant he touched her. At the moment there was nothing—*nothing*—she wanted more than Boone. Everywhere. In every way. Forever and ever and ever.

And if he was just joking with her now—if it turned out that this was nothing but a game he had no intention of following through to its obvious conclusion—she'd kill him. She'd tear him limb from limb with her bare hands and feed his remains to Mack.

But as she stood before him in nothing but her bra and panties, she received the distinct impression he had no intention of putting a halt to what he had started. In spite of that, she was cautious as she drew near him again.

In his uniform, with the patches on his sleeves and the captain's insignias on his collar, and with his broad shoulders straining at the seams of his shirt, his heavy biceps vaulting against his sleeves, he was just so big, so overpowering, so...so...so *masterful*, she thought. The stark white fabric of his shirt made his eyes seem greener, brighter, somehow. The sunlight winked off of his badge in a spark of silver and ignited his hair with gold, as if a white-hot wildfire burned perpetually at his center. She had never known a man more compelling. And she was helpless not to obey his command.

This time, when she stood on tiptoe to kiss him, she curled one hand around his neck and opened the other over his chest. His heartbeat raged fiercely beneath her fingertips, the shuddering violence of it almost too much for her to bear. When she felt her knees begin to buckle, she wound his shirt in her fist to keep herself standing. Boone reciprocated by roping his arms around her waist to aid her. Then he skimmed one hand down over her fanny, discovered that what she was actually wearing was a thong bikini, and groaned long and loud.

"Oh, Lucy," he bit out, cupping his hand more intimately over the bare flesh of her bottom. She felt him grow stiff and lusty against her belly.

His fingers curled into her skin and brought her hips forward, and, too excited now to do otherwise, she rubbed herself sinuously against him. He gasped and his eyes fluttered closed, and for a moment she feared he would push her away. Then he dropped his other hand to her taut fanny, insinuated his thigh between her legs and dragged his pelvis solidly against her hip.

The friction of his hard leg moving between hers was too much for Lucy, and her knees finally failed her. She circled his neck with both arms, fairly climbed him until her mouth was even with his, then pressed her lips to his in the kiss that he had demanded. His hands on her bottom gripped her more tightly, lifting her until she could wrap her legs around his waist. Boone held her there for a long time, his body still, his heart pounding, utterly passive as she plundered his mouth with hers.

Then, suddenly, he wasn't passive at all. He caught the back of her head in one hand, tangling his fingers in her hair, pulling her head back to expose the creamy skin of her throat. He opened his mouth against her neck, rubbing his slick tongue over her flesh, nipping and laving her tender skin. The hand cupping her fanny lifted her higher, and he dipped his head lower, burrowing between her breasts.

This time Lucy was the one to gasp when he covered the peak of her breast with his mouth, suckling her through the lace of her brassiere. His hands fumbled for a moment with the closure at her back, then the wisp of red raspberry went tumbling to the ground. She was fully exposed to him as Boone's ministrations became more insistent. He pulled her nipple into his mouth and sucked hard, his motions demanding and unceasing.

Lucy buried her fingers in his hair and pulled him closer, murmuring soft sounds of encouragement as he tasted her more deeply still. She was halfway aware of motion, but didn't realize where he was taking her until she felt the cool cotton comforter beneath her back. Boone followed her down, his mouth still fastened to her breast, his big body crowding hers backward until the swell of the pillow at the head of the bed stopped them.

She felt his hand between her legs and realized that at some point he'd removed her panties. He scored the damp, heated core of her, petting her, palming her, penetrating her, moving deeper and more intimately with every stroke. Lucy moaned and writhed wildly beneath him, oddly exhilarated that she was naked and he was still fully clothed. Nevertheless, that wasn't going to work out for what she wanted to do to him.

Reaching between their fiercely thrashing bodies, she jerked at his belt until she'd managed to free it, pushed the annoying barrier away and unfastened his trousers. Then she slipped her fingers inside to caress him, her hand traveling down and down and down. Her eyes widened in wonder when she realized he was so...oh...

At the intimate touch, Boone stilled. He lifted his head from her breast and caught her gaze with his, the hand buried in the folds of warm skin between her legs continuing to stroke her idly. Lucy met his gaze levelly, circled him more completely with her fingers, then dragged her thumbnail slowly along his hard length.

He closed his eyes and moaned, then removed his hand from her with obvious reluctance in order to circle her wrist. With strong fingers, he gripped her, guiding her hand back and forth against himself. Lucy watched fascinated as his expression melted from arousal to near ecstasy. Then his eyes snapped open and, with clearly even more reluctance, he carefully moved her hand to his shirt.

"Now take off my shirt," he told her, the words dry, rough and strained.

She complied immediately, slipping each button through its hole, marveling at the expanse of hard, tanned muscle and soft gold coils of hair revealed with the opening of each one. When she finished, she spread the sides of his shirt open wide and silently bade him to rise enough for her to shuck it off his shoulders. Then she bent to place a chaste kiss over his heart, tasting his heat with the tip of her tongue. But he wound his fingers in her hair again and gently pulled her head back so that she could look at him.

"The pants, too," he told her.

Lucy smiled and moved lower, tugging his trousers and briefs over his muscular hips and lean thighs, down along taut calves. He toed off his shoes when she got to his ankles, then she removed his pants completely and tossed them to the ground. When she turned, she found him watching her, his eyes lit with a barely subdued fire.

"On your back," he told her.

Her heart skidded to a halt, then hammered double-time. She complied with his command, lying at the center of the bed, her eyes fixed on his. For a long time Boone only stared at her, his gaze traveling from her face to her torso to her legs. Then he splayed his hand open over her belly, moving it slowly, casually, up to cover one breast.

"I've never had a slave in my bed before," he said softly, pinning her with his gaze.

Lucy tried to chuckle, but only seemed to manage a strangled little sound that bore no resemblance whatever to the real thing. "I find that hard to believe."

He shook his head slowly, and his gaze wandered down to where he gently palmed her breast. "You'll really do anything I tell you to do?" he asked her.

She hesitated for a moment, biting her lip in thought. Then, slowly, she nodded.

"Anything?" he asked again, still not looking at her face.

"Yes."

He smiled, the gesture turning his expression absolutely feral. "Oh, boy."

Leisurely he caught her nipple between his thumb and forefinger, rolling it gently before softly squeezing her soft flesh. Lucy closed her eyes and held her breath and wondered how long he was going to prolong her needful agony before giving her what *she* wanted. For long moments he toyed with her breasts, then she felt his fingers skim down along her body. He tucked his hand between her legs and urged them apart, then the mattress shifted beneath her as he left her side.

She opened her eyes and mouth to protest, then realized he hadn't left her at all, but had simply taken up a much more intimate position, supplicating himself before the hot, dewy heart of her. Before she could utter a word, he bent his head to taste her, his mouth wreaking pleasure on her like none she'd ever experienced before. Helplessly she closed her eyes and twisted the sheet in her restless fingers, begging him to stop what he was doing at once, then entreating him to make it last forever.

And just as "forever" seemed to come, Boone moved away, only to return immediately to cover her body with his. He caught both her wrists in one big hand and lifted them over her head, holding them gently but firmly against the pillow above her. Lucy opened her eyes to find him towering over her, his smile at once menacing and accommodating, his heart pounding rapid-fire against her own.

"What would you have me do now?" she managed to ask, wondering where she found the strength.

He lowered his head to the curve of her neck and shoulder, kissing her lightly, nuzzling her with his jaw. "I want you to cancel any plans you've made for the afternoon. I don't have any classes today, and all the things I have in mind to do instead could take a while."

She grinned weakly. "Done."

"And then," he said, his voice dropping an octave, "I want you to enjoy yourself. Like I intend to enjoy you."

Before she could comment, he moved again, this time insinuating his hips between her legs, spreading them wide. Then, still holding her wrists captive in one hand, he rose up on his knees, silently commanding her to circle his waist with her legs. When she did, her hips rose off the bed, and he shifted once before plunging himself deep inside her.

She felt him everywhere. When he entered her with one long thrust, he seemed to touch every part of her. Lucy groaned aloud at the invasion, but helplessly opened herself to him even more. It had been so long....

So long since she had shared such an intimate union with another human being. So long since a man had made her feel so deeply feminine, so wonderfully beautiful, so utterly wanted. So long since she'd felt the stirrings of love for another living creature, an emotion that had been such an infrequent companion in her life. There weren't many people whom Lucy had loved. And because of that, when she did love, she loved fiercely. Totally. Irrevocably.

She hadn't meant to fall in love with Boone. But now, with him inside her—both physically and emotionally—she knew he would be with her forever. Emotionally forever, at least. The physically forever part would have to be up to him.

Her thoughts evaporated before they could become fears, because Boone began to move again, a slow, steady rhythm that was both primitive and tenacious. Instinctively she thrust her hips forward, claiming even more of him, and heard him growl her name in response. Then the cadence of his passion began to accelerate. He pelted her relentlessly, and she reveled in the storm. She cried out his name as he emptied himself inside her, both of them shuddering at the force of his completion.

Only then did Lucy realize what she had done. She'd allowed him inside her without taking any precautions. No barrier, no protection, nothing to keep her safe. Yet oddly, it wasn't the threat of any physical repercussion that alarmed her—even without the recollection that, cyclewise she was in no way fertile at the moment. What she knew she had endangered most in her neglect was her heart. Her soul. Herself.

But her fears again dissipated when she felt Boone shift his weight from atop her to nestle his big body alongside hers, pressing his front to her back. He draped an arm over her waist and pulled her close against him, settling his chin affectionately on her shoulder, covering one of her legs with one of his. Their bodies were slick and warm with the remnants of what, for her anyway, had been a loving union. Lucy did love Boone. She knew there was no question about that. And no matter what the outcome of this new development in their relationship proved to be, that part of it would never change.

She opened her mouth, halfway intending to tell him how she felt, when he stirred a little behind her. "I think I could get used to having a slave in my bed," he said softly.

Only in your bed? she almost asked him. But something checked the question before she could utter it. Something that told her she didn't want to know the answer.

"Lucy?"

She inhaled deeply before responding to Boone's quiet query, unwilling to have the tremor in her thoughts emerge in her voice when she spoke. "Yes?"

"There are a few other things I want to do with you." He paused a meaningful beat, then, "And *to* you."

Her heart hammered hard in her chest, and a strange fire overcame her entire body as he whispered in her ear the most erotic, illicit, uncompromising acts.

"You won't mind, will you?" he asked, his voice low and languid.

She shook her head slowly. "Of course not," she whispered, the shiver in her words only mimicking the one that wound through her body. "I am, after all, your slave. And I'll do anything for you."

What had she done?

Lucy lay in bed in her motel room the following morning and asked herself that question and a dozen more. What had come over her at Boone's house the day before? How could she have spent an entire day—*an entire day*—in a man's bed doing all those things to him? How could she have let him do all those other things to her? How could she have let herself enjoy it *so much?*

And how could she have slipped out just before sundown, while he was asleep, without giving him an explanation or saying goodbye? She hadn't even left anything in the oven for his dinner, she remembered. Some slave she'd turned out to be.

Her face flamed when she recalled the intimate details of yesterday afternoon. No one had ever come close to making her feel the way Boone Cagney had made her feel. How could something like that happen? She had barely known the man three weeks. How could he have her so tied up in knots in such a short period of time? Was she really that desperate? That lonely? How could she have given herself over to him in such a blatant, damn-the-consequences way?

Yesterday Boone had somehow made her forget who she was. Completely, irrevocably. She had done things with him she would never have considered herself capable of doing. And he had roused things in her—feelings, desires, *needs*— that she hadn't even realized she had. He had turned her into a person she barely recognized. How was she supposed to pay off the rest of her debt without losing herself to him completely?

Because on top of everything else, she still had to finish paying him back for saving Mack's life. The debt was only half-paid—she still owed him two weeks of slavery. Of course, she hadn't initially planned on providing him with all the services she'd provided yesterday, so she supposed she could call that a major bonus, consider them even, and never go back to his house again. He had, after all, been telling her since the beginning that he didn't want her around. Of course, that had been before...

Before she'd become his love slave.

Now she had no idea what he wanted from her. Or if he still wanted her at all.

Lucy groaned and whirled over on the mattress, jerking the sheet up around her naked body. The action was vicious enough to bounce Mack right out of bed, and he landed on the floor with a brief thump and an angry howl.

"Sorry," she grumbled. Then she rolled back over again and glared at him. "No, I'm not. Where were you yesterday? Why didn't you do something to stop all that...you know. I mean, you had to have heard us. It's not like we were even trying to restrain our..."

She groaned again at the memories and left the statement unfinished. Mack blinked his green eyes and frowned at her.

"You were probably hiding in the basement, weren't you? Look, I know you find the mating habits of humans unsightly and prolonged, but the least you could have done was turn over a lamp or the china cabinet or something. Anything to coitus interrupt us."

Her attempt at levity didn't faze him. He looked away, in the direction of the kitchenette, and said, "Mrff."

Lucy rolled her eyes to the ceiling and kicked off the covers, then rose naked from bed and reached for her robe. "How you can be hungry at a time like this eludes me."

Mack padded after her as she filled a motel ashtray with cat food and set it on the floor before him. He squatted and curled his tail around his body, content to munch for some time. Lucy sighed while she watched him eat and wondered how he could be so complacent. At least she listened sympathetically when *he* had problems in *his* love life. Of course, having been the one to have him neutered, she supposed his lack of a love life was all her fault, anyway.

"Dammit," she muttered under her breath. "What am I going to do now?"

She settled an elbow on her knee and propped her chin in her hand, thinking intently and assessing the situation. Okay. Maybe things weren't as bad as she thought they were. So she and Boone had made love. So what? It wasn't like she was some trembling virgin who didn't know what to do next. People had sex all the time. Not her, of course, but other people. And it wasn't that big a deal to them, was it? No, it was not. Therefore, it shouldn't be a big deal to her. Right?

Oh, sure.

So what she and Boone had engaged in had been wild, jungle monkey love of the most primitive, carnal variety. So what? It had still been basically no different from any other sexual experience she'd ever had, and it didn't necessarily mean anything. Right?

Yeah, right.

And okay, so it was going to be a little awkward when she showed up at Boone's house this morning to try and explain something that she didn't for a moment understand. She had a good fifteen minute drive from her motel to his house— twenty if she stopped for coffee and Danish, which now that she thought about it, sounded like a very good idea. Surely she'd come up with something plausible by then. Piece of coffee cake. Right?

No problem.

But none of her reassurances to herself were anywhere near reassuring. She showered and dressed halfheartedly, and as she gathered up Mack and locked the motel room door behind them, she told herself to stop worrying and to just do what she had to do. Unfortunately she quickly realized that what she *had* to do actually shared very little in common with what she *wanted* to do. What she *had* to do was finish paying up a debt she owed to Boone for carrying Mack to safety. Period. What she *wanted* to do...

She felt a warm ripple of need creep through her body, pooling in a place deep inside her where she hadn't felt warmth in a long, long time—not before yesterday, anyway. What she wanted, she told herself, she had better stop thinking about for a while. Because it didn't seem likely that Boone was ever going to give it to her. Not on her terms, anyway. Not for any length of time.

Nevertheless, for some reason, she couldn't quite shake the feeling that the repercussions of his saving Mack's life extended far beyond retrieving her cat from a burning building. In many ways, by saving Mack's life, Boone had saved Lucy's life, too. Which meant she really had not one, but two debts to pay. And all she could do was wonder just how long it was going to take her to settle that additional debt.

Eight

Lucy arrived at Boone's house nineteen minutes and zero ideas later. Fortunately for her, Boone himself was nowhere to be found. When she didn't see his car in the driveway, she strode to the garage and peered through the dusty glass on the door, thinking it would probably be there. But she saw no sign of it.

She checked her watch. Just past eight. She knew he didn't have another shift at the station until tomorrow morning, and he normally worked his other job in the afternoon. And seeing as how cranky he always was whenever she came over at this hour, it seemed to her there was little chance he'd be up at this time of day if he didn't absolutely have to be.

So just where was he?

She fished his front door key out of her pocket and wondered why she should suddenly feel sheepish about using it to enter his unoccupied house, when she'd been doing so without compunction for two weeks now. This was her normal routine, she reminded herself. Show up with breakfast, share it with

Boone, then go to work on his house. Why should today be any different from the fifteen that had come before it? Obviously Boone had risen and gone out to meet the day as if nothing in the world were any different than before. So why shouldn't she?

"Hello-o-o?" she called out when she pushed the front door open. "Anybody home? Boone? You here?"

Mack trotted in from behind her and headed straight up to Boone's bedroom, just as he did every day, also obviously unconcerned that anything should be different today. Lucy shrugged, figured she must be taking things too seriously if Boone and Mack were so utterly unconcerned, and tried to ignore the little stab of...what?...disappointment?...that jabbed at her heart. Something cool and weighty uncurled in her stomach, and she closed the door behind herself with a quiet click.

Well what had she expected? she wondered. That Boone would have been as emotionally moved by what had happened yesterday as she'd been? That he would be waiting here for her this morning with French toast and champagne mimosas and a bubble bath drawn for two? How could he know what yesterday had meant to her? she berated herself. How could he know that there had been no one in her life since her marriage had dissolved? How could he know that the feelings he'd aroused in her completely obliterated the now laughably feeble feelings she'd had for her husband? And how could she have assumed that he would consider her anything special?

She sighed again. Apparently she wasn't. She was just a lowly slave.

She closed the door behind herself and tried to remember what she had planned to do today before getting so, um...sidetracked...yesterday. The hall closet, she remembered after a few distracted moments. She had been planning a search and seizure mission on that thing. As it was now, it could barely be closed, it was so crammed with junk.

A little over two hours later, Lucy was hip-deep in Boone's past and had almost managed to chase memories of yesterday from her mind completely. How one human being could amass so much *stuff* was beyond her. It was as if every time something broke down or went bad, Boone just tossed it into the hall closet.

Among other things, she'd dug up one unstrung racquetball racquet, most of what was left of a battered sneaker, a Swiss army knife that was more corkscrew than anything else, a half-dozen broken umbrellas, a beat-up 1978 yearbook from Hoover High School—which, Lucy recalled, her softball team had knocked out of the state championship finals twenty years ago—a variety of machine hoses of undetermined origin, and just about the ugliest Hawaiian shirt she'd ever seen.

Oh, yeah. And a framed photograph of Boone holding on to a beautiful woman as if he never intended to let her go.

That last item Lucy had placed on the floor near her feet, leaning it haphazardly against the wall, where she could look upon it continuously and batter herself senseless for her own stupidity. Obviously this was Boone's ex-fiancée, the woman he had once loved enough to want to keep her with him forever. The one he quite possibly *still* loved enough to want to keep her with him forever. Lucy paused in her activities and picked up the photo again, studying it more closely this time, even though she'd already memorized every detail.

Boone was standing behind his fiancée with his arms draped over her shoulders, and she had lifted both hands to cling to the strong forearms that Lucy herself had so frequently fantasized about holding on to forever. The woman was what one might call a classic beauty—petite and delicate looking, with long blond hair, wide blue eyes, a sunny smile, a narrow waist and surprisingly full breasts. She wore a dainty flowered blouse, and her hair was held in place by an even daintier velvet headband. Tasteful gold bracelets adorned both wrists, rings circled several fingers—including a rather large diamond on the fourth finger of her left hand—and a thin gold chain with a heart-shaped locket hung around her neck.

She could have been the poster child for every archaic view of the weaker sex. Something about her just screamed, ''I am woman—hear me titter prettily and give me no-fat dressing on my salad, 'kay?''

But it wasn't the woman in the photograph that bothered Lucy. What bothered Lucy was the image of the man standing behind her. Boone's expression was completely open, completely carefree, completely happy. He was smiling in a way she had never seen him smile and looked like a man who had just been given everything he could possibly ever want. He looked like a man about to embark on the dream of a lifetime. He looked like a man irreversibly in love.

So this was the kind of woman who could bring out unbridled joy in him, she thought, gazing at the blonde in the photo again. Certainly Lucy had never seen a reaction even remotely like this from him when he was in her presence. Of course, she supposed she hadn't given him much to feel supremely happy about. She'd invaded his life without invitation. She'd turned his home into her own dream house, subconsciously replacing the one she'd lost when she wasn't able to find anything on the market to her liking. She'd enslaved herself to the man in the basest way possible without even considering how morally questionable he might interpret her actions to be.

Worst of all, she was nothing like the kind of women he evidently favored. Oh, sure, she might have provided him with hours of fun in the bedroom, but clearly, when it came to a forever-after kind of love, Boone wanted an entirely different sort of woman.

Just like everyone else in her life had.

Lucy sighed and pushed the melancholy thought away. No sense getting maudlin. It's not like she hadn't expected something like this to happen. On the contrary, this fit the pattern of her life perfectly.

The front door opened behind her without warning, and Boone appeared on the other side in a slice of sunlight, each arm roped around a paper grocery sack. Thanks to the glare of the sun, Lucy couldn't quite make out his expression, but his whole body seemed to stiffen when he saw her standing there.

"Hi," she said automatically. "You're out early."

He seemed to relax a little at her benign salutation, but continued to stand motionless at the threshold, as if he wasn't quite sure he was welcome in his own home. "I couldn't sleep," he said softly. "So I went down to the Y to work off some steam. Then I had a few errands to run."

Lucy decided it might be best not to comment on that steam-working-off business and said instead, "I was just cleaning out your hall closet." Belatedly she realized the remark was unnecessary, because the scattered collection of items at her feet was probably a pretty good clue as to her activities. And of course there was the previously discarded photograph of him and the love of his life that she held in her hands.

"What happened to you last night?"

Boy, nothing like getting right to the point, she thought. She dropped her gaze down to the picture of Boone and his fiancée and felt something twist a little painfully in her chest. "I, um…" She sighed heavily, then forced herself to glance up at him again. But she still couldn't quite make out his features, thrust into shadow and obscured by the glare of the sun as they were, so she really didn't know what to say. "I had to go," she finally finished lamely.

"Where?" he demanded. "I woke up, and you were gone."

She studied the floor. "Yeah, I know. I'm sorry. I just…I had to go," she repeated.

Boone took a few steps into the house and kicked the door closed behind him. Lucy didn't *look* like a dirty, double-crossing witch, and she certainly wasn't acting like one, but then neither had Genevieve. He studied closely for a moment the woman who claimed to be his slave and wondered what had happened yesterday to chase her from his house without a word of explanation.

After the afternoon they'd spent together, he'd been looking forward to a pretty eventful night. But he'd awakened after dark to find himself alone on one side of the bed, and an empty indentation still warm and redolent of Lucy on the other. She'd left him without even saying goodbye. Just like Genevieve had.

But where Genevieve had never returned—neither to apologize, nor to explain—Lucy had come back to his house this morning, just as she did every day, and she'd gone to work, just as she did every day. By the looks of her, nothing between the two of them had changed as a result of their lovemaking yesterday. And frankly, that had Boone stumped. Because regardless of his own reason for and reaction to what had happened yesterday, he'd had Lucy pegged as the kind of woman who would have read a lot more into it than there actually was.

And just what, exactly, had there been to it? he asked himself for perhaps the hundredth time since waking to find her gone. He was no closer to an answer now than he had been the first time he'd considered it. One thing was certain, though. Whatever was going on between him and Lucy was unlike anything that had ever happened to him before. He just wished he knew what she thought about it.

Then he dropped his gaze to her hands, hands that seemed to be worrying with an inordinate amount of concern whatever it was she was holding. He tilted his chin toward what looked like a framed photograph. "What have you got there?"

Immediately she tucked the picture behind her back. "Nothing. Just something I dug out of your closet."

"It looks like a photograph."

"It is."

Boone smiled. Probably something from his past that was going to embarrass him profoundly. "What?" he asked again, a smile playing about his mouth for the first time since yesterday. "Come on, let me see it."

"No, it's nothing," she said with an anxious shake of her head. "I'll just put it with the other stuff, and you can go through it later. After I'm gone. When you're alone."

He set the groceries down on the floor and extended his hand toward her with a grin. "Come on, Lucy, give it to me. I'm not going to be embarrassed by a photograph." He smiled again. "Not unless it was one taken during my mustache phase. That damned thing never would grow right."

Again she shook her head. Her unwillingness to release the photo puzzled him. Hell, it was *his* pride at stake, not hers. "Lucy," he said, adopting his most authoritative tone of voice. "Don't make me say it again. Hand it over. Now."

She arrowed her eyebrows down in clear anxiety, but slowly brought her hands around from behind her, then gingerly extended the photograph toward him. Boone was still smiling when he took it from her, but when he glanced down and discovered the subject of the picture, he frowned.

Dammit. He thought he'd managed to completely eradicate every scrap of evidence that even hinted at Genevieve's presence in his life. How the hell had he missed this? The photo had been taken shortly after they'd become engaged. He'd been wildly, deliriously, blindly in love, overcome by the prospect of a future that held nothing but promise.

Promise. Yeah, right. He'd actually been convinced that Genevieve would keep her word to him. He'd actually been certain she would love him forever. He'd actually thought she could be trusted. What a sap he'd been back then.

He glanced up at Lucy, who was staring intently at something over his left shoulder. Good thing she was, too, he thought, because lately he sure as hell seemed to be forgetting to watch his back.

"Is that…your fiancée?" she asked without looking at him.

"Ex-fiancée," he said.

Lucy nodded. "She's beautiful."

He expelled an errant chuckle and nodded back, unable to deny that Genevieve was indeed that. "Yeah, she was a looker all right. A real lady," he added, forcing the bitterness out of his voice. In that respect, at least, he added to himself, unwilling to reveal to Lucy or anyone else how badly he'd been duped by his former love. "Schoolteacher, churchgoer, art lover," he added for his own private torture, the irony that such an embodiment of beauty and goodness had turned out to have traces of neither in her system.

He thought Lucy nodded again, but the action was so subtle, he wasn't sure. "You, uh…you really loved her, huh?"

Unfortunately Boone couldn't deny that part, either. "Yeah. I really loved her."

"That's nice," Lucy said, her voice sounding small and distant. "It's good when people fall in love."

"Maybe," he conceded with some distraction, his thoughts returning to that day in the church, when he'd spent hours waiting for a dream that never showed up. "But it sure as hell won't happen again. Not to me. Not in this lifetime."

When he looked at Lucy again, she was gazing directly at him, her expression a strange mix of something he couldn't quite identify. He noted absently that she was garbed in her usual cleaning-out-something attire—baggy overalls, baggier sweatshirt and heavy hiking boots—and remembered that she drove a truck and earned her living as a roofer. And inevitably he found himself comparing her to the woman he had once intended to make his wife.

Genevieve had taught second grade. She had worn flowered dresses and high heels, and cardigan sweaters draped over her shoulders, clipped together at the collar with one of those chain things that were staples of elderly aunts and librarians. Her hair had been waist-length and blond, she'd always taken about half an hour to put on her makeup, her jewelry had been elegant and ample, and she'd always smelled like a big basket of flowers.

Lucy Dolan, on the other hand… Boone sighed his confusion. Lucy smelled like a soap commercial and dressed like a construction worker. Hell, she was a construction worker. And she was about as feminine as a pit bull. How the hell had he managed to become so consumed with hot, heavy dreams about and desires for a construction worker? Something about her roused his libido more fiercely and rapidly than any woman ever had. Something about her drew him fast, drew him furious, drew him deep. And all he could do was fight like hell to keep himself from becoming so lost with her that he never found his way back.

Because in spite of all their differences, there was one thing Lucy did have in common with Genevieve—the ability to wreck his life completely. This time, however, he was prepared. This time he was going to stop the train before it ever got near the end of the tracks.

He saw her drop her gaze to the floor, where he'd set the two bags of groceries. "I just went to the grocery store for you," she said, her voice sounding soft and oddly empty.

He bent to scoop the bags up again, then started toward the kitchen. "You forgot to buy steaks."

Her answer came from behind him, at a pace that told him she was barely able to keep up with him. "Actually," she said, "I didn't buy any on purpose. Red meat really isn't good for you. Once in a while is fine, but you're such a meat and potatoes man, Boone, and I just figured chicken and fish would be much more—"

"And you forgot the Oreos, too," he interrupted her.

She hesitated a moment before replying, "Well, again, although it's fine in moderation, too much sugar can be bad for you. As it is, you have to have something sweet every mor—" Her voice clipped off for a moment, then she added a little more heartily, "And that can lead to all kinds of health problems."

"And I needed a few other things, too," Boone told her.

Like condoms, he thought, trying to stifle the hysterical laughter he felt welling up inside him. He'd actually been thinking that he and Lucy might have another session like the one they'd enjoyed yesterday, and he'd wanted to be prepared for it this time. What a laugh. What a hoot.

What a jerk.

No way would he let things go that far again. No way would he set himself up for another fall like the one that had nearly crippled him two years ago. No way would he let himself feel anything more for Lucy than an idle curiosity about how she might perform sexually, a curiosity that he had more than satisfied yesterday.

No way.

Yesterday he'd forgotten himself for a while. He'd forgotten what could happen to a man who let down his guard and assumed things he shouldn't. Lucy would only be hanging around in his life for a little while longer, then she'd bug out on him. Why make things more difficult for himself than they were already?

He placed the bag of groceries on the table, then turned to shrug out of his jacket. He hung it on a peg by the back door and spun around again, just in time to see Lucy sorting through the first of the grocery sacks.

"You don't have to do that," he said hastily, rushing back to the table to stop her.

"That's okay," she said, reaching back inside. "I'll put these things away. Why don't you go relax for a while?"

He ignored her suggestion and instead tried to remember which bag the condoms were in, then realized he had no idea. Lucy removed an industrial-sized bag of potato chips, frowned at him and said something about pretzels being much better for him than all that greasy stuff, then reached back inside. Boone was extending a hand to stop her when she plucked her own hand out of the bag, her fingers curled possessively around a box of condoms. A *big* box of condoms. Her cheeks were flaming when she looked up at him.

"They're not for you," he blurted out.

In spite of the awkwardness of the situation, she smiled. "Yeah, I kinda figured." She glanced nervously at the box, then back at Boone. "They're not my size."

"No, I meant—"

"Maybe we should talk about what happened yesterday."

He drew a ragged breath and held it, then told her softly, "It won't happen again."

Had he not known better, he would have sworn she flinched at his reassurance. Considering the way she had ducked out on him without a word last night, he would have thought she would be glad to hear that. Instead she seemed disappointed. Oh, well. He guessed women were entitled to enjoy a good time in the sack as much as men traditionally did. He didn't flatter himself that he was anything extraordinary in that department, but yesterday had been rather...remarkable. It was only normal for the two of them to regret that they would never experience something like that again. Not with each other anyway.

"Look, Lucy," he tried again, "it never should have happened in the first place. Things got a little out of hand. I had no right to ask you, or rather to *tell* you, to—" He stopped abruptly, reminded himself that they'd both been willing participants, and tried again. "All I can do is promise you it was a one-time thing."

She nodded, her mouth set in a tight line of grim resignation. "A promise isn't worth much coming from a man who doesn't think anyone on the planet can keep their word."

Okay, so she had a point, he ceded. "Then forget about my promise. Just know that what happened yesterday won't happen again."

"You're right," she said. "It won't."

Well, that was easy, Boone thought. Why wasn't he intensely happy about receiving such a quick and agreeable response from her? Before he could stop himself, he asked, "It won't?"

She shook her head resolutely. "No. It won't. Yesterday was...was..." He couldn't mistake the faintly wistful smile that curled her lips, however briefly it appeared. "Yesterday was wonderful," she admitted. "But you're right—it was also a mistake. Obviously we both agree about that, and obviously we're going to take care that nothing like that happens again. Enough said."

Actually, Boone thought, not nearly enough had been said. But he couldn't quite decide what more to add. And he supposed she had a point. If neither of them had any desire to engage in such a pastime again—and clearly it had been nothing more than a pastime to either of them—then there was no reason to sit around yakking about it. But if that were true, then why did ending the discussion now make him feel so...incomplete?

"Enough said," he agreed reluctantly.

She glanced down at the box of condoms she still held in her hand, then extended it toward him. "Here. Don't spend it all in one place."

His reply was automatic. "Don't worry. I won't."

She nodded. "That's what I figured."

"Lucy..."

"I brought some apple turnovers," she interrupted, turning away from the sack before she even finished emptying it, leaving the scattered groceries where they sat on the table.

It wasn't a good sign, Boone thought. Lucy never left anything unfinished.

"I can reheat them if you're interested," she added. "They're really not as good as *I* could have made them, but they're passable."

If that was the way Lucy wanted to play it, Boone thought, then that was the way they'd play it. For now, at least. He couldn't quite shake his conviction that there was still much unsettled between the two of them, but he supposed right now wasn't a particularly good time to analyze the situation. So he only stood there and regarded her with silence.

She must have taken his lack of response to mean he was amenable to breakfast, so she crossed to where she had set the bag of turnovers on the counter. "These can be ready in about fifteen minutes," she said as she began to arrange them on a cookie sheet. "Hot and sweet, just the way you like it in the morning."

When Boone still said nothing in reply to her chatter, she turned to look at him again. "What?" she asked. "You don't want store bought? Okay. I could whip you up something homemade, but it's going to take a while. If you're not that hungry—"

"Oh, I'm hungry," he said, eyeing her levelly. "I'm just not sure..."

He sighed fitfully, suddenly wanting to be well and truly rid of her for some reason. Lucy had turned his life upside down from the moment she'd arrived at his front door. She'd roused feelings in him he'd sworn off long ago, and she'd reminded him of a time when his life had been a whole lot more enjoyable, a time he'd forbidden himself to recall. In short, she was making him do things he'd *promised* himself he would never do again. Just how much longer was she going to hang around being a nuisance before she decided she'd paid her debt and walked out of his life for good?

One month, a little voice in the back of his head reminded him. *She said she was your slave for one month, and she's going to give you one month. She* promised *you.*

Yeah, yeah, yeah, he replied silently to himself. For what that was worth. Exactly zip.

"Well?" Lucy said, calling him back from his reverie.

"Well, what?" he asked shortly, having forgotten what they were talking about.

"Do you want me to fix you something homemade? Tell me what to do. I'm your slave, remember?"

As if he could forget, Boone thought. "I don't care what you do," he told her. "Hell, I didn't even know you could bake."

She narrowed her eyes at him, and he wondered what he'd said to make her so angry. "Of course I bake," she retorted, her voice frosty. "It's one of my favorite things to do. I even won a blue ribbon at the Virginia State Fair six years in a row for my chocolate chip cookies."

"Is that a fact?"

He silenced himself soundly before blurting out that chocolate chip cookies were one of his greatest weaknesses. That would be just what he needed—for Lucy to have him at her mercy even more completely than he already was.

Dammit. Now he was angry, too. For no reason he could rightfully name, either.

She nodded with determination. "Starting when I was ten years old."

"Well, isn't that just the cutest thing in the world?" he bit out.

Her frown intensified. "Yeah. Ain't it though?"

Lucy glared at Boone, reminding herself he couldn't possibly understand why his challenge of her culinary abilities made her so mad. Nevertheless, she wasn't about to tell him. Unexplained, unfounded resentment served him right, she thought. He deserved it for being so in love with a woman who wasn't even a part of his life anymore. A woman who was soft and beautiful and demure, and who completely overshadowed anyone who might dare to take her place. A woman who'd made it impossible for him to ever fall in love again.

Lucy felt Boone's curious gaze on her as she flipped open cabinets and began to withdraw all the fixings for turnovers. But she tamped down the urge to explain to him that baking had been the only thing she'd ever enjoyed that had won her parent's approval in some small way. Earning awards for making cookies had been suitably little girlish enough for her mother and father to actually praise her on those occasions when she'd taken ribbons at the fair, so Lucy had baked her heart out for them.

Unfortunately being a good little baker still hadn't been enough to pay them back for taking her in to begin with. Because they'd continued to remind her on a regular basis how grateful she should be that they hadn't left her in a state-run facility to rot.

And baking obviously wouldn't be enough to win Boone over, either. But then she hadn't expected that it would be. She was just relieved to see that he wasn't going to say anything more about what had happened yesterday. Then she was immediately and irrationally perturbed by the fact that he could so easily forget about the tumultuous afternoon they'd shared. Then she made another quick about-face and envied him for his convenient lapse of memory.

Lucy spun around and gripped the kitchen counter behind her and gazed fiercely at the man who had her so tied up in knots. Finishing out her indenture was going to be the hardest thing she had ever done in her life. Because regardless of the fact that he was in love with another woman—the kind of woman Lucy would never, ever be—and regardless of the fact that there was absolutely no future in anything that might develop between them as long as he felt that way, and regardless of the fact that she had already lost more of herself to him than she could really afford to lose...

Regardless of all those things, Lucy still wanted Boone with all her heart. But she simply would not—could not—live her life again with the knowledge that the person she cared most about in the world didn't want what she was. It would slowly destroy her to feel the way she did about Boone knowing he would never feel the same way about her.

She swallowed hard and remembered again that she still owed him two weeks. Two weeks of seeing him on a regular basis and falling more in love with him. Two weeks of being forced to face the fact that she would never be more than second best to him. Two weeks of being reminded daily of the exquisite perfection of the one afternoon they had shared, and the absolute knowledge that she would never experience such joy again.

Two weeks had never seemed like such a lifetime.

Oh, yeah, she thought as her gaze roved hungrily over every inch of him. Keeping her word and paying this particular debt was going to be a real challenge. And suddenly Lucy felt very, very tired.

"Um, Boone?" she said quietly. "Would it be okay if I took the day off from slavery today?"

His posture changed dramatically at the question. His eyes fairly sparked with anger, his gaze fierce and penetrating, pinning her to the spot. "Take the day off?" he demanded, clearly upset by her request.

She nodded. "Yeah. I'm really...I didn't sleep well last night, either," she said by way of an explanation. "And I could use a rest."

"A rest," he echoed.

She nodded again. "Just for today. I promise I'll be back tomorrow."

"Oh, and of course I can take you at your word on that, can't I?"

She wished she could understand this hang-up he seemed to have about promises. But all she said was, "Yeah. You have my word."

His eyes held hers for a moment, then darted to her mouth, her breasts and points beyond. Lucy felt heat burn her body everywhere his gaze fell, until all she wanted to do was strip naked to relieve the fever—and a few other discomforts as well.

She closed her eyes tight and pinched her fingers over the bridge of her nose, more in an effort to keep herself from looking at Boone than to ward off the headache she felt threatening. "Look," she tried again, "if I don't get some rest, I'll—" She bit off the words quickly when she realized she'd been about to reveal that if she didn't get some rest, she'd be all over him like white on rice.

"You'll what?" he asked, his voice still tinted with that sarcasm she didn't understand.

She sighed and squeezed her eyes closed more fiercely, and only then did she realize it was because she wanted to cry. And there was no way she was going to let Boone witness a display like that. "Let's just say I'll probably do something I'll regret later," she said quietly. "Can I please just have the day off? Please?"

He stood stoic and silent, staring at her, his hands resting on his trim hips, his jaw clenched tight. His entire body reflected his taunting anger. "Yeah, you can have the day off," he finally said. "Hell, take two weeks if you need it."

She drew in a shaky breath. "That won't be necessary. I'll be back tomorrow."

"Yeah, I just bet you will."

He punctuated his response by moving aside, so that nothing impeded her path to the kitchen doorway. Growing more and more depressed with every passing moment, Lucy didn't even bother to straighten up the kitchen and left the turnovers and baking supplies right where they sat on the counter. She whistled for Mack, who came obediently within seconds, and scooped him up to clutch him close to her heart.

Then she breezed past Boone as quickly as she could, being careful not to brush up against him or get any closer than she absolutely had to. Not because *she* didn't want to touch him, but because *he* seemed so anxious not to touch her.

As she yanked open the front door, her gaze was drawn to the photograph on the floor of Boone embracing his fiancée, and, inescapably, she recalled his reaction to it. He had referred to the woman in the photograph as a real lady. Lucy smiled sadly. To him, that obviously meant not dressing like a man, not working like a man, not acting like a man. Evidently Boone liked his women to be…girls. And Lucy had never been one of those.

For all she knew, his fierce response to her yesterday had simply come about because he was desperate and aching and lonely for the woman whom he had once intended to make his wife. The last thing Lucy needed or wanted was to get involved with a man who wanted someone else, someone different, someone she would never in a million years be. It had hurt badly enough to be a disappointment to her parents, and later to her husband. Only a fool or a masochist would bring something like that on herself again. And Lucy was neither of those. Well, not a masochist, anyway. And only foolish for other reasons.

Unfortunately when she recalled the way Boone had been watching her in the kitchen only moments ago, with a level gaze that was at once empty of emotion and full of fire, she began to wonder if she might just be both stupid and crazy after all. Because all she'd wanted to do was make love to him again, regardless of the fact that the only reason Boone had ever made love to her in the first place was because she had been convenient.

And she wondered yet again how she was going to make it through the next fifteen days.

Nine

Boone had no way of knowing whether or not Lucy would return to his house the following day as she'd promised, because he had a shift to work at the station. Normally, however, she arrived before seven with his breakfast and was busily invading his space by the time he left. But the morning after she'd told him she needed the day off, by the time he left his house at seven forty-five, he'd heard not a word from her.

Typical, he told himself as he locked the front door behind himself and made his way to the garage. He'd known from the start that she wouldn't keep her word. So why was he so surprised by her absence? She had been no more capable of keeping her promise to him than anyone else had ever been. End of story, close the book on that one, move along to the next chapter of life. He ought to be enjoying some satisfaction that he'd been right about her all along.

So why wasn't he satisfied? he asked himself. Immediately, an answer came to him. Because, dammit, Lucy was supposed to have been different.

The thought jarred him to a halt in front of his garage. Was that true? he wondered. All this time, while he'd been telling himself Lucy was just like all the other people who'd broken promises to him in his life, had he actually been hoping she'd be the one to prove him wrong? Why?

He shoved the unanswerable questions away. The point was moot now, because she hadn't proved him wrong. She'd bugged out on him without seeing her promise through to the end. She wasn't coming back. If she were, she would have been here by now.

And why was he complaining, anyway? he demanded of himself. He'd wanted her out of his life, and she was. He'd expected her to go back on her word, and she had. Everything had worked out exactly as he had wanted it to, exactly as he had known it would. Now his life could go back to normal. He should be feeling relieved, overjoyed, satisfied.

Unfortunately Boone felt none of those things. What he felt was…restless. Uncertain. Incomplete. It was an odd sensation, and he wasn't quite sure what to make of it.

He glanced down at his watch. On top of everything else, he was running late. So, pushing his errant thoughts away, he heaved up the garage door, climbed into his car and headed off to work. He wished he could hope for a busy day to keep thoughts of Lucy at bay. But he couldn't even do that. Because a busy day for him meant tragedy for someone else. And he wasn't quite selfish enough to indulge in something like that.

So, knowing he was probably doomed to be preoccupied by memories of wide blue eyes and raspberry-colored panties for some time to come, Boone backed out of his driveway and drove to work, telling himself that nothing had to change. He would continue to live his life the way he had before—freely, mechanically, carelessly, independently.

And alone. Blissfully, gloriously alone. Just the way he always wanted to be.

But when he turned down his street the following morning, Boone was surprised to find himself still expecting Lucy to be at his house. Surely he'd been mistaken yesterday morning when he'd been so quick to assume that she would go back on her word. Surely something as simple as a traffic jam or broken alarm clock had prevented her from arriving at her usual time. Surely he'd go home to find that she'd paste-waxed his hallway without telling him, and the moment he stepped out in his stocking feet, he'd go careering forward and break his neck.

Surely she was there waiting for him with a hot breakfast and a warm smile, just as she had been for the past two weeks.

But her truck was nowhere to be seen when he pulled into his driveway. And his house looked completely undisturbed. Boone parked in his garage and let himself in through the back door, just as he always did. And immediately he missed the two sounds he'd become accustomed to hearing in greeting— Lucy's off-key singing and Mack's unholy howl.

Man, he must be suffering from something serious, he thought, if he was missing that damned cat.

Boone shrugged out of his coat and hung it in its usual spot. Then he turned around and noticed a scrap of yellow paper on his kitchen table that he couldn't recall leaving there himself. And he realized that Lucy had been at his house, after all. He tamped down the swell of something raw and unwarranted in his belly, brushed aside the stub of pencil that still sat on the note, and read:

Boone,
I'm sorry, but I'm going to have to finish up my slavery in shifts. There's a new subdivision going up in Ballston, and my boss said the work's there for me if I need it. And I do need it—I finally found a house I like, but it's going to cost more than I planned.

And I've decided to take your suggestion and hire a private investigator to look for my brother. That's going to cost money, too. Still, if it means finding my family, it's worth it, right?

If it's okay with you, I'll hang on to your house key

and come when I can to work off the fifteen days I still
owe you. It may take a while, but I'll get them in. I
promise you I will.

There are three loaves of blueberry banana bread and
some carrot-raisin muffins in the freezer for your breakfast. That should get you through the week. I'll leave
dinner in the fridge on the days I come by.

See you when I see you.

Lucy

And that was all she wrote. Boone bit back the ironic laughter that threatened to overtake him at the appropriateness of
the cliché.

Okay, so she'd come back, he thought. For one day. Big
deal. She'd only done it to tell him she wouldn't be making
good on her promise after all, because she was going back to
work before paying off her debt to him. Oh, sure, she was
going to come back for fifteen odd days to pay him back. Oh,
sure, she was going to be his part-time slave until her full
indenture had been worked off. Oh, sure, she would make
good on her promise. Oh, sure.

More likely, she'd show up for a few more perfunctory
visits, then disappear from his life completely once she had
her own life up and running again.

He picked up the note and scanned it once more. Her handwriting was angular and uniform, in no way similar to the
uneven, loopy circles he normally associated with feminine
handwriting—like Genevieve's had been. Lucy had written
that she'd found a place of her own. So *of course* she wouldn't
be coming back to his house. Because now she could paint
her own walls pink. Now she could put flowered bedspreads
on her own bed. Now she could plant things in her own windowsills. Obviously she didn't need Boone's house anymore.

And obviously she didn't need Boone.

Because she was going to look for her family, too. She was
going to find someone else to need, someone else to be needed
by, someone else's life to meddle in. Boone was off the hook.

Free and clear. In one quick, easy motion, he had everything just the way he wanted it. Lucy was gone, and his house—and his life—were his own again. No one invading, no one underfoot, no one being a nuisance. Just him. All alone. By himself. Just the way he liked it.

"Damn straight," he muttered under his breath.

His words seemed to echo in the empty air surrounding him. And for the first time he could ever recall, Boone thought about maybe getting himself a dog.

The house in Arlington was almost everything Lucy had hoped to find. A three-bedroom, two-bath, scaled-down Tudor, with a fireplace in the living room, built-in bookcases in the master bedroom, a sprawling maple in the front yard and bedding for plants in the back. There was a tidy little patio for barbecuing, a two-car garage to provide plenty of room for storage—not that she had anything to store—and a white wicker swing on the front porch that just begged a person to sit there and read and sip a glass of wine once the weather turned warm again.

Already Mack had staked out his spot in a splash of sunlight that dappled the walk between the branches of the maple, and Lucy laughed lightly as the big tomcat rolled and rolled as if he were just this side of heaven. Something in the ivy beneath the front shrubs alerted his attention, and he dove swiftly to sack whatever unsuspecting prey was about.

She stood at the curb, leaning against her truck, and simply drank in the sight of her new house. She could paint the rooms any color she wanted. She could throw as many violets or fruit baskets as she cared to on the bed. She could arrange the furniture, then rearrange it, then rearrange it again to her heart's desire, and no one—no one—would come home and yell at her. The place was almost perfect. There was just one thing missing.

Boone.

His face materialized in her mind before she had a chance to stop it, and instinctively she squeezed her eyes shut to chase the image away. But no matter how hard she tried, Boone Cagney wouldn't leave her alone. Even though it had been two weeks since she'd seen or spoken to him. Two weeks since they'd enjoyed the kind of sexual encounter she'd only thought possible in fevered dreams.

Two weeks since he'd told her he would never, not in this lifetime, fall in love again.

Since then Lucy had managed to work off four more days of her slavery. But only on days when Boone had a shift at the station. She didn't want to risk running into him in the flesh. Because his flesh was simply too tempting for her to bear.

Eleven more days, she told herself. Only eleven more days to spend at his house, and she'd be done.

Why didn't the realization bring her more satisfaction? How come she found no joy in the prospect of making things even between them, when her conscientiousness in paying off debts was the one thing in life in which she'd relentlessly taken pride? All she'd lived for, since losing her home to fire, was to pay Boone back for saving Mack's life. Now she was closer to doing that. So why wasn't she happier?

She sighed and pushed herself away from the truck, then strode casually across her front yard. Marigolds along the front walk come spring, she planned halfheartedly. Pansies around the lamp post. Black-eyed Susans along the chimney. Artemisia along the hedge. Too bad spring was a good five months away. She could have used the distraction.

The house was empty and had been for months, so her steps echoed hollowly as she crossed the hardwood floor in the living room. Dust tickled her nose, so she opened a few windows as she passed them, to invite in the crisp November breeze and to air the place out. She wanted to move in as soon as possible, as soon as she could round up some furniture and have it delivered. Living in a motel for the past six weeks had been less than comfortable, and she was tired of eating all her meals from the grocery store deli.

Well, of course, she hadn't eaten *all* of her meals from the grocery store deli, she recalled as she ascended the stairs to the second floor. There had been quite a few times when she'd shared them with—

She halted at the threshold of her new bedroom and expelled an impatient sound. Would there ever come a time in her life when she would stop being blindsided by thoughts of Boone? For some reason, she doubted it. That was the problem with people like her, who'd had so little experience with love. Once they fell, they fell hard. And often they never got up.

She sighed and began to make plans again. Cherrywood furniture in the bedroom, she thought. Maybe a nice deep blue on the walls. And maybe she'd go back for that fruit basket comforter. The blueberries in the print would go so nicely with Ocean Mist....

Boone never knew when Lucy was going to strike—he only knew she would come to his house at times when he wasn't around. And he could always tell immediately after walking through the door whether or not she'd been there. If she hadn't been there, his house felt empty, silent and cold. And if she had...

If she had, the house always felt inviting, welcoming and warm. Even without her actual physical presence, she made the place seem homier somehow, just by having occupied it briefly. It got to the point where Boone found himself returning home after a shift with more anticipation than he'd ever felt for anything in his life.

Had she or hadn't she? he'd always ask himself just before turning onto his street. And, more important, would this be the morning when he caught her before she got away?

Because there were times when he was convinced that Lucy did her work by night, fleeing in the early hours before his shift ended, before the sun even rose, like some spry little cobbler's elf. But she always managed to elude him. He'd rush into a house filled with the sweet aroma of something freshly baked, and find a kuchen or Danish ring, still steaming and fragrant, sitting at the center of his kitchen table.

And beside it, a note from Lucy. Always a note from Lucy.

"Your hot water heater should be fine now. Just a minor adjustment or two…"

"Dinner's in the fridge. It's a lentil casserole. Trust me, you'll love it…"

"Sorry about the tear in your uniform pants. Mack got a little carried away. The stitches hardly show at all…"

"Only one more day to go, and we'll be even…"

One more day, Boone marveled, on a cool, crisp Tuesday in the middle of January as he read over her most recent missive. She was really going to do it. She was actually going to finish out her slavery. She was honestly going to keep her word to him, in spite of the many obstacles she'd had to face, more than a few of which had come about because of Boone's behavior.

The realization that she was going to make good on her promise to him when no one else in his life ever had should have amazed and astounded him. Instead, he found himself wondering how he ever could have doubted her.

And wondering just what he was going to have to do to make up for distrusting her.

Now who had a debt to pay? he wondered. How was he ever going to make amends for having essentially called Lucy a liar from the beginning? What did a man do to compensate for continuously comparing a perfectly nice woman to a perfectly selfish one, when he'd had no foundation for doing so?

Because it suddenly occurred to Boone that that was exactly what he'd been doing ever since meeting Lucy. Even after two years, he still had this misguided idea stuck in his head that his ex-fiancée was the definitive example of womanhood, and that any female would be exactly like her.

Which made Boone feel doubly stupid, because from the beginning, all he'd done was compare Lucy to his ex-fiancée, and always he'd marveled at how very different the two women were. So how come he'd had Lucy pegged in the same hole Genevieve had occupied? How come he'd assumed she'd be exactly like his ex, when in fact she'd never shown any sign of any similarity?

Why? he asked himself again. Because you're an inconsiderate, dim-sighted imbecile who's still obsessed with the woman who wronged you, when you should be besotted with the one who's made you feel good for the first time in years, that's why.

Boone wanted to throttle himself silly. After all this time, he was still letting Genevieve make his life miserable.

No, not Genevieve, he told himself. She hadn't been around for years. Boone had been the one responsible for keeping the anger and suspicion alive, for nurturing it and wallowing in it and letting it blind him to any potential happiness he might have found otherwise. For two years he'd let it prevent him from trusting other people, from caring for them, from loving them.

Although that wasn't exactly true, either, he thought. Because he was also beginning to understand that, try as he had, he hadn't quite been able to keep himself from falling in love with Lucy. And he called himself a fool for having taken so long to realize it.

Now what? he wondered. He folded the note neatly in half and stashed it in a wire basket atop the fridge alongside the others from Lucy. She was already moving along nicely in her life without him. Hell, he didn't even know where to find her. By now she would surely have moved into her new house. For all he knew, she may be on the verge of finding her family. Just how long did it take to locate a long-lost brother?

She still owed him one day, he reminded himself. If nothing else, Boone knew he had that coming to him. Unfortunately he had no idea when that day would be. It could be this week, or it could be next. Depending on her work schedule, it might take a month. But Lucy would be back. Of that he was certain. He just had to make sure he was there when she was. Otherwise...

Otherwise, he'd be the one hiring a private investigator to find a lost love.

* * *

Boone felt like an idiot staking out his own house. But that's exactly what he did for the next two weeks. He traded shifts with one of his brothers at the station, in spite of the bad luck associated with such an act—too many firefighters had been injured or even killed when working a trade—and the even more likely threat that payback would be hell—whoever he traded with would be able to pick the day he wanted to have the favor returned. Boone felt it likely that he'd be enjoying the next few holidays down at the station.

On those mornings he stayed home when he should have been out fighting the red devil, he rolled his car out of the garage and parked it two blocks away, then hoofed it back to his house to lie in wait. Whatever it took to catch Lucy in the act. Four days into week two of playing the spy, Boone did just that.

He was upstairs in his bedroom, flipping through the latest issue of *Fire Engineering*, when he heard her truck rumble into the driveway. Immediately he closed the magazine and sat motionless, lest the slightest sound give him away. The front door opened and closed with a faint creak behind her, then her heavy boots thumped down the hallway below. Before Boone could move, he heard a soft padding on the stairs that led to his room, and, too late, he remembered Mack.

As soon as the cat's memory vaulted into his head, the cat himself topped the last stair. At first he didn't notice Boone. Not until he leapt up to the bed and turned to make himself at home. Then he arched into an angry posture, narrowed his eyes and howled. Loud and long and lustily.

"Mack?" Lucy's voice came from downstairs, touched with alarm. "What is it? What's wrong?"

Panicking that Lucy would leave before they had a chance to talk, and unmindful of the repercussions to his person of what he was about to do, Boone reacted instinctively. He rushed the cat and tackled him, then rolled onto his back on the bed and pinned the animal to his chest. By hugging the beast close, he managed to limit the thrashing and clawing to a few minor scrapes and a lot of angry growling.

"I have the cat!" he called down to Lucy. "And if you ever want to see him again, you'll do exactly what I tell you to do!"

Silence was his only reply for a moment, followed by a wary "Boone? Is that you? What are you talking about?"

Mack lurched against him as Lucy ascended the stairs, and another struggle ensued. Boone jerked his head back when the cat freed one paw and took an angry swipe at him, barely missing a slash on his cheek. The two of them were still wrestling on the bed when Lucy covered the last stair and found them.

"What on earth is going on up here? Mack? What do you think you're doing? Let Boone go."

Boone had been under the impression that *he* was the one holding Mack, but now that Lucy mentioned it... He was on his back with the cat sitting atop him, claws penetrating his sweatshirt and sunken nicely into his chest. Mack's eyes were wide and feral, and his lips were curled back into what Boone could only describe as the satisfied smile of a hunter who has but one blow left before rendering his prey senseless. Mack seemed just about to do so when Lucy pulled him off Boone and set him on the floor.

"Go pick on somebody your own size," she told the cat, shaking a scolding finger at him. Then she turned to Boone. "What are you doing here?"

He jackknifed up from the bed and rubbed his hand where he was certain Mack had tried to bite off a finger. "I live here," he said.

"You're supposed to be at work."

"And you're supposed to be my slave."

"Only for one more day."

"Yeah, well, I still have the right to claim that day."

She crossed her arms defensively over her chest. "Meaning?"

"Meaning..." He sighed heavily and deflated some. "Meaning I've missed you, Lucy. Where have you been?"

Something hot and tingly sizzled in Lucy's midsection at

Boone's quietly uttered declaration. But she tamped it down before it had a chance to ignite. So he'd missed her, she thought. Missed all the libidinous things he'd done to her, he meant. Missed all the salacious things she'd done to him in return. Missed the kind of erotic explosion the two of them had shared that one afternoon. Who needed to be missed as a plaything?

Unfortunately, in spite of her realization that he'd only missed her on a purely sexual level, Lucy couldn't deny how wonderful it was to see him again. With his unruly curls tumbling down over his forehead and his heavy-lidded gaze lingering on parts of her that hadn't felt warm for weeks and his muscular forearms visible beneath the bunched up sleeves of his sweatshirt, and his mouth just begging for the caress of a woman's lips....

She swallowed the sigh that rose in her throat. He was even more handsome than she remembered him being. And her memories of Boone, if nothing else, were as clear and as vivid as sunlight bursting through finely cut crystal.

"I've been busy," she said evasively.

He nodded. "Yeah, I know. Moving into a new house, finding your family, dodging me."

"I haven't found my brother yet," she said softly. "The private investigator I hired is still working on it. He said it could take a while." She felt her face heat as she added, "And I haven't been dodging you."

"Haven't you?"

She dropped her gaze to the floor and shook her head silently.

"Funny how you only seem to come over on days when I have a shift at the station and can't possibly be here."

She lifted one shoulder halfheartedly, then let it drop again. "Our work schedules don't seem to jibe," she said. "It's just a coincidence."

"Right."

She snapped her head up and met his gaze levelly again.

"So what are you doing home today? You're supposed to have a shift."

"I've been trading off with one of the other guys for a couple of weeks."

"Why?"

"Because I wanted to see you, and I couldn't think of any other way. I mean, you steal in here like a thief, and all that's left of you by the time I get home is the aroma of a freshly baked something that's hot and sweet. Not that that's such a bad thing," he quickly amended, "especially when it's chocolate chip cookies." He smiled devilishly. "But I'd rather have you. The winter has been so unseasonably cold, and I have so much trouble keeping warm."

She forced a smile. "Try flannel sheets. I think you can find them in plaid. Probably even in that icky brown and gold combination that you like so much."

His smile softened some. "Like I said, I'd rather have you."

In spite of how foolish she knew it would be to set herself up for such a thing, Lucy immediately decided that being Boone's love slave for one more day had a certain... oh...attraction to it. A sort of beguiling...fascination. A rather intriguing kind of...allurement...an enticing—

"Boone," she interrupted her own thought processes, hoping she just imagined the little squeak in her voice, "we've already been through this. It's pointless to go over it again."

"You're still my slave. You owe me one more day."

"But—"

"You promised me, Lucy. You *promised.*"

She drank in the sight of him as he lay on his bed, taking him in detail by detail as her gaze roved hungrily over his body. The broad shoulders, solid chest and trim waist that his baggy sweatshirt somehow enhanced, the narrow hips, strong thighs and salient calves that strained against his blue jeans, the bare feet—a male body part Lucy had never found sexy until Boone had come along. And the arms. This time she couldn't stop the sigh that sifted between her lips. Because Boone's arms were just too delightful for words.

"Lucy?" he asked, his voice indicating his puzzlement with her lack of response.

"Hmmm?" she murmured dreamily.

"You're still my slave for one day, right?"

Helplessly she nodded.

"Well, then."

Without further hesitation, she lifted her hands to the top button of her flannel shirt and began to unfasten the bindings one by one. Well, she had promised, after all, hadn't she? And if keeping her promise meant she had to spend another day engaged in an unutterably explosive sexual encounter with the man she loved, well then, that was just the price she'd have to pay, wasn't it?

She was surprised to see Boone go a little white when she started to unfasten her buttons. She was even more surprised to see him blush furiously when she jerked her shirttail out of her jeans. But when she began to pull her shirt off her shoulders and he abruptly sat up and cried, "Wait!" she really got confused.

She halted her actions and pulled the shirt back on, leaving it hanging open over the demi-cups of a sapphire-colored brassiere. "Wait?" she echoed. "For what?"

Boone scrambled off the bed and stood before her, then took the shirt from her hands. As her bewilderment compounded, he closed the buttons one by one with trembling fingers, until her shirt was fastened up to her neck.

"That...um...that's not...uh...what I was going to tell you to do," he stammered softly.

Lucy slumped forward, gaping, her anguish and disappointment an almost painful thing. "It's not?"

He cleared his throat a little roughly, then said, "No."

"But—"

"Not yet, anyway."

"Then what...?"

He sighed, covered her shoulders with his hands and smiled. "You're still my slave, right?" he asked again.

She nodded. "Yes."

"You still have to do what I tell you for one more day, right?"

"Yes."

He squeezed her shoulders again, his smile growing a little nervous for some reason. Then he cleared his throat once more and said, "Lucy?"

"Yes, Boone?"

"Kiss me."

"But I thought you said you didn't want—"

"Kiss me," he repeated more forcefully, his smile growing a little more relaxed. "Now."

As she had, too many weeks ago to remember, Lucy cupped her hand around his neck, stood on tiptoe and pressed her mouth to his. Softly, chastely, swiftly. Then she stepped back. "Okay, I kissed you. Now what?"

Boone reached for her, pulled her toward him until her body was flush against his and gazed down into her eyes. He opened his mouth, as if he were going to say something, then closed it when he seemed to change his mind. For a long moment he looked at her curiously, then finally he spoke again. "Stay with me," he said simply.

Lucy's heart shivered for a moment, then began to pound wildly against her ribs. "What?"

"Stay with me," he repeated. "After you've worked off your enslavement, don't be so quick to run off."

She eyed him suspiciously, wondering if he was asking her what she thought he was asking her, then immediately assured herself she couldn't possibly be interpreting his statement correctly. He couldn't possibly be asking her to—

"Why?" she asked.

"Why?" He hesitated briefly, lifting his hand to stroke her hair. "Because we're good together, you and me."

In spite of the sentiment, she couldn't quite convince herself that what he was saying was a good thing. "In what way?" she asked further.

His eyes widened in obvious surprise. "How can you even ask that after the afternoon we spent together?"

She nodded slowly, feeling the lurch of her stomach all the way to the bottom of her soul. Just as she had suspected. So Boone wanted her. And being wanted—honestly, truly wanted—was just about the most important thing Lucy could imagine. Except for being loved. And, unfortunately, the two were in no way mutually inclusive. Evidently it was possible, after all, for Boone to *want* a woman other than his ex-fiancée. He just couldn't love one.

"Yeah, we were good together that day," she agreed reluctantly. "But there's no way I can stay with you, Boone."

His expression would have been the same if she had kicked him in the shin—startled, confused, hurt. "Why not?"

"Because," she told him, feeling a cold lump settle somewhere between her stomach and her heart, "you don't...want me."

He gaped at her as if he couldn't believe she'd just said that. "Of course I want you. You're—"

"No, you don't," she said, unwilling to have him clarify what she already knew to be true. "Not the way I want to be wanted." She swallowed hard and then said more quietly, "Not the way I *need* to be wanted. You've told me yourself a million times that you don't want me here."

His whole body seemed to sag forward. "Lucy, that was before. Before we—"

"It's still not right, Boone. It's still not..."

He looked so confused. Lucy sighed, feeling more disheartened. It was yet something else to reinforce how completely different their individual takes on the situation were.

"Not what?" he asked.

She pushed herself away from him and took a few steps backward, stopping at the top of the stairs. "You want me?" she asked him, her throat nearly closing over the last word.

"Of course I want you. I just told you I did."

She nodded. "See, that's where the problem is. Because I *love* you, Boone," she said softly, marveling at the change that overcame his features when she said the words aloud that had lingered for so long in her heart. "And it wouldn't be an

even trade,'' she added sadly. "Loving someone means wanting them—and needing them, too. But wanting doesn't necessarily include loving. Or needing, either, for that matter. So
you wanting me and me loving you…it would be a totally
unbalanced relationship. You'd wind up owing me.''

He said nothing in response, only stood at the center of his
bedroom staring at her, as if he couldn't believe she'd just told
him what she'd just told him. Lucy couldn't blame him. She
could hardly believe she'd voiced her feelings out loud herself.

"And we've already discovered that one of us being in-
debted to the other doesn't work very well at all.''

There was no way she was going to be able to finish up her
slavery today, Lucy thought. Working with Boone in the
house, after revealing to him what she'd just revealed, after
having made a fool of herself by offering herself to him and
then telling him it would never be enough, having just *exposed*
herself to him, both physically and emotionally…

It was just too much. It hurt too bad. He was gazing at her
as if she were the most pathetic creature he'd ever had the
misfortune to encounter. His eyes were filled with disbelief,
disappointment, discontent. He looked like a man who wanted
to be anywhere but there. Which was pretty bad, she thought,
considering the fact that this was his home.

Or at least, it had been. Before she'd come in and messed
everything up. For both of them.

"I have to go,'' she said suddenly.

"Oh, no you don't,'' he countered just as quickly. "Not
this time, Lucy. Not like that.''

She took another step backward, lowering herself into the
stairwell. There were so many things she wanted to say, so
many things she wanted to tell him. But to do so would just
make things worse, she knew. It would only serve to open up
more of herself to injury, and embarrass Boone in the process.
It was bad enough she had admitted to loving him. No way
was she going to further humiliate herself by vowing that she
would do so forever.

"I have to go,'' she repeated, descending another two stairs.

Boone took a single step forward. "You can't go," he insisted. "You still owe me a day."

"I'll pay you back later."

"You'll pay me back today. Lucy, that's an order."

She shook her head quickly and moved down another two stairs. "I can't."

"You have to."

Another step down brought her to the landing. She looked up at the top of the stairs to find Boone standing there glowering at her. "Don't you understand?" she said, not entirely able to squelch the little sob that punctuated the question. "I can't, Boone. I *can't*."

It was all she could do not to burst into tears on the spot. In a last-ditch effort to save what little dignity she had left, Lucy turned and half ran, half stumbled down the remainder of the stairs. She whistled to Mack and lunged for him the moment he came into sight, then she fled through the front door without a backward glance. She didn't even bother to strap the cat into his carrier. She simply set him on the seat beside her, ground the engine to life, and careered backward down the driveway in a haze of white exhaust.

Only then did Lucy allow herself the luxury of crying. On top of everything else, she thought, with a stifled sniffle and swift swipe of her nose, she'd been so close to fulfilling her obligation to Boone. And now that she'd acknowledged to both of them how she felt, she knew she wouldn't be able to come back and pay off the debt. Not in a million years. It would be too hard, too humiliating, too hurtful.

It was just one more reason that Boone Cagney would haunt her for the rest of her life.

Ten

At 8:30 that evening, Lucy was already dressed in her pajamas and ready for bed. Not that she actually ever *slept* in pajamas—she was a restless sleeper and didn't like to be confined by something like clothing—but they were nice for lounging around before turning in. In this case they were over-size, flannel and decorated with various international travel destinations. She had rolled the legs up to her knees, pushed the sleeves up past her elbows and left the top hanging open over a white tank undershirt beneath.

She sat cross-legged on the floor of her new living room, not just because she liked sitting on the floor, but because, even after almost two months of living in her new house, she had yet to decide on what kind of furniture to buy. Every time she went out looking, she realized everything she liked was already sitting in Boone's house—the color schemes, the fabrics, the styles. No matter how hard she tried to find something different, she kept remembering how much she'd liked the touches she'd given to his home better.

Mack was curled up in her lap, and Stevie the bear was tucked under one arm, the three of them watching "My Man Godfrey" on cable and working their way methodically through a pint of Cherry Garcia ice cream—well, she and Mack were, anyway. She glanced down at the cat purring in her lap and smiled, then ruffled him affectionately behind the ears, grateful for the big black tomcat's reassuring presence.

"Okay, one more bite," she told him, spooning a small portion of pink onto the carton lid for his enjoyment. "But that's it. Dr. Greene would kill me if she knew I was letting you eat ice cream."

Mack licked his lips and eyed Lucy reassuringly, as if to tell her he wasn't about to reveal their secret.

"And it's only because we're wallowing in self-pity, got it? It's only because we're trying to forget all about Boone and how much he's come to mean to us."

Mack was too busy eating to acknowledge her question right away, and instead kept his head buried over the ice cream. When he finally looked up, he gave his mouth a thorough going over with his tongue and said, "Mamf."

"Okay, okay," she conceded. "*I'm* trying to forget how much he's come to mean to *me*."

She was about to comment further when a quick rapping at the front door halted her. She glanced briefly down at her pajamas, decided she didn't care one way or another how she looked, then set the empty ice cream carton on the floor beside her. When she gently lifted Mack from her lap, he grumbled something unintelligible in complaint, but he curled up quietly beside the ice cream container without further argument. Lucy stroked her palm down the length of him as she rose and went to answer the door.

There were a couple of people Lucy could have anticipated would come calling. But Boone Cagney wasn't one of them. Especially not Boone Cagney holding a bouquet of multicolored carnations in one hand, and a store-bought birthday cake with candles blazing in the other.

Standing in the hazy yellow glow of the bug light outside,

he looked almost unearthly somehow. His cheeks were stained pink by the winter wind, the same wind that had also ruffled his unruly curls about his head in much the way Lucy would herself, if given the opportunity to touch him again. She inhaled a shallow breath to steady her suddenly rampaging pulse rate, and detected a lingering trace of cold, dry air and wood smoke that surrounded him.

"Happy birthday, Lucy," he said softly, the greeting sounding rough and reluctant, as if it were someone else's idea, and not his, to be standing there offering it. In spite of his tone of voice, however, he was smiling. It wasn't a big smile, granted. But it wasn't bad.

"Thanks, but it's not my birthday," she replied automatically, too befuddled to say much of anything else.

"Can I come in?"

Wordlessly she stepped aside to let him enter, then closed the door to the night chill that threatened to follow him inside. She had no idea why he would show up here looking for *her.* Especially accompanied by flowers, warm wishes and candlelight. Not after the way she had deserted him earlier that afternoon, and not after what she had revealed to him.

Unless, of course, he still intended to collect on that final day—or night—she still owed him.

She absorbed him detail by detail as he entered, appreciating yet again how well his clothes clung to him. His snug jeans lovingly molded his trim hips and lean legs, and his broad shoulders strained at the seams of what appeared to be his high school baseball jacket—decorated with letters from not just baseball, but track and football, as well.

Lucy remembered, then, that she was dressed in her rumpled oversized pajamas and big socks. Oh, boy, she thought. She was in no way dressed for the occasion. Whatever that occasion turned out to be.

When Boone spun around and caught her ogling him, she closed her eyes tight, as if the pretense might convince him that she hadn't really been staring at him, honest she hadn't. But when she opened one eye experimentally and saw his single, idly arched brow and the soft smile playing about those perfectly exquisite lips, she knew that he knew how thoroughly she'd been taking inventory. And she felt a blush creep up from her heart to her hairline.

Not certain she could trust her legs to carry her, Lucy leaned against the front door behind her, her hands pressed flat at the small of her back. Without much success she tried once more to slow her heart rate with a deep, unsteady breath. Unfortunately, when she saw the way Boone was gazing back at her, her pulse only accelerated.

"What are you doing here?" she asked him.

He glanced back over his shoulder toward the television that was still blaring loudly. Carole Lombard was trying to convince William Powell how much he needed her, and neither was seeing the other's point of view at all.

"No furniture?" he asked when he saw the state of things. His voice bounced eerily around in the vacant quarters.

Lucy shrugged awkwardly. "I haven't quite found anything I like." She snapped her mouth closed before she added, "As much as I liked what I did with your place, anyway." Somehow she didn't think either of them needed to be reminded of how foolishly she'd behaved in that respect.

He turned back to study her in silence for a moment, then seemed to remember he was there for a reason. "Is there someplace I can put this?" he asked, inclining his head toward the birthday cake. "I don't want to burn your new house down." That mysterious smile emerged again as he added, "We'd have to call the fire department."

"Looks to me like the fire department's already here," Lucy noted, still unnerved by his presence and still unable to pinpoint exactly why.

"Yeah, well…" he hedged. "Not in a professional capacity." He eyed the burning cake a little dubiously. "Not yet, anyway."

Her curiosity and discomfort finally getting the better of her, she pulled the sides of her pajama top closed, crossed her arms defensively over her abdomen and blurted out, "Just what *are* you doing here, Boone? And how did you find out where I live?"

He wiggled his eyebrows playfully. "We firefighters have access to these things," he said mysteriously.

She narrowed her eyes at him. "And what makes me think that gaining such access for personal reasons is a trifle, oh…unethical?"

"Hey, we're obligated to protect and serve the local citizenry," he said, easily sidestepping the question. "It's our job. Not to mention our calling."

"And just what kind of protection and service are you thinking about offering me tonight?" Lucy asked warily. "I sure didn't call you."

Instead of answering her, he only smiled and brought his hands toward each other again, indicating his burden once more. "The cake?" he asked pointedly.

Lucy pushed herself away from the door, trying to ignore the fact that her legs felt like banana peels as she moved toward him. "Put it in the kitchen," she said, waving her hand in that general direction. When the action caused her pajama sleeve to fall down past her fingertips, she shoved it back up to her elbow impatiently.

"You'll have to excuse my state of dress," she told him as she strode across the living room toward the kitchen. "I wasn't expecting anyone. To what do I owe the honor?"

He followed her closely, then set the cake, its candles still burning merrily, at the center of her kitchen table, and laid the flowers beside it. He was quiet while he shrugged out of his jacket and hung it on the back of a chair. Then he met her gaze levelly and said, "I came over to wish you a happy birthday."

"It is *not* my birthday," she repeated. She bit back a sob that was both angry and sad. "My birthday was months ago. Don't you even remember?"

He nodded, his jaw set firmly. "Oh, I remember."

Lucy pinched the bridge of her nose, squeezed her eyes shut

and willed back the tears she felt threatening. ''Then what's with the cake?''

When she opened her eyes, Boone was pushing the sleeves of his long-sleeved, charcoal-colored T-shirt up to his elbows to reveal strong forearms that drew her gaze like a magnet. Inevitably she recalled again that hazy night months ago when he'd carried her to safety. And with all her heart, she wished she could turn the clock backward just one time. If only things could have been different between them, she thought. If only.

He lifted the flowers from the table again, then, in a half-dozen strides, crossed to where Lucy was leaning back against the counter. He stood towering over her like some big, blond Adonis, and for a moment, her heart nearly stopped beating. But it kicked up again—albeit erratically—when he smiled and said softly, ''Happy birthday, Lucy.''

''But it's not my—''

''Yes, it is,'' he interjected gently.

''No, it isn't.''

''As far as I'm concerned it is.'' He sighed in exasperation and dropped the flowers to his side. ''Humor me, okay? Let's go back in time a few months and pretend this is your birthday. Because I have a present for you.''

His words about going back in time echoed her own thoughts and startled her for a moment, and all she could do was stare at him and wonder what was going on. It wasn't her birthday. And even if it had been, she would have been spending it alone. She'd never shared her annual celebration with anyone other than the twin brother from whom she'd been separated, and only in a vague, hazy, halfway neurotic manner at that.

But she'd shared her birthday with Boone last month, she reminded herself now. She'd gone to his house to barbecue dinner and wound up the recipient of just about the best birthday present she'd ever been given—that mind-scrambling kiss from Boone. The one he had called *harmless* and *innocent*, the one Lucy had considered neither.

She had told herself at the time that her reason for going to

Boone's house on a day where she normally sequestered her-self away from society was simply because her debt to him far overshadowed the observance of an annual tradition. She had assured herself then that her birthday was unimportant in light of the near tragedy Boone had prevented. She had gone to his house because she owed him, nothing more.

Now, however, she was beginning to wonder if maybe her whole reason for embarking on that evening hadn't simply been specifically because she was growing tired of being so alone. And not just on her birthday, either.

But that still didn't explain why Boone was here now, in-viting himself to share in what was, for her, the most intimate of all experiences. And he was wishing her happiness, some-thing that should be so easy to achieve. Something that had eluded her for so long.

"Are you with me on this?" he asked her.

She gazed at him blankly. "On what?"

He expelled an impatient breath. "Can we do like at the movies and suspend our disbelief for a little while? Can we make this your birthday?"

"Boone, I have enough trouble getting through one birthday a year. Why would I want to have another one?"

"Because this one will be happy. I promise."

She chuckled wryly. "Oh, sure. And we all know how se-riously you take promises, don't we?"

He eyed her intently for a moment. "Okay, I deserved that. Just indulge me, all right?" he asked again.

Although the thought of indulging Boone took on an en-tirely different meaning in her head than she supposed he in-tended, she nodded reluctantly. "Okay. It's my birthday," she muttered halfheartedly.

He straightened and held out the flowers to her again, a smile of triumphant satisfaction lighting his face. But Lucy only continued to lean against the counter, her arms crossed resolutely over her chest, sullen and silent.

"Aren't you going to make a wish and blow out the candles?'' he asked her, when she made no move to acknowledge his gifts.

A wish? Lucy wanted to ask him. For what? There were so many things she wanted, so many things to wish for. She wanted her life back in order after losing virtually everything she had to a fire and a man who didn't love her. She wanted to know what had happened to a brother she couldn't even be positive she had. She wanted a family again. She wanted to love and be loved by someone. She wanted to be wanted. She wanted to feel whole. She wanted far too many things to ever have them all.

And blowing out the candles on a birthday cake wasn't likely to give her any of them. Dammit, she hated birthdays. Why had she let Boone talk her into this one?

"Um, no," she said. "I don't think I will."

He gazed at her, nonplussed. "Why not?"

"Because wishing never solved anything, that's why. Wishes never come true."

Boone studied Lucy closely. She'd been so jovial, so good-natured since he'd met her. She'd been nothing at all like the distant woman who stood before him now. She'd even watched her home burn to the ground dry-eyed, he recalled, and had been so grateful to have saved next to nothing. He couldn't imagine anything that would sober such a person so thoroughly. Except maybe thinking she was unloved and unwanted by the man she wanted and loved.

"At least take the flowers," he told her, giving the bouquet in his hand a little shake. "Unless you're also averse to accepting presents on your birthday."

She drew in a small breath and released it in a quiet sigh, then reluctantly accepted the carnations. She touched them cautiously with her fingertips before removing them from his hand, as if she wasn't quite sure how they should be handled. Then she wrapped her fingers carefully around the stems, lifted the blossoms to her nose for an idle sniff and smiled sadly.

Boone watched as she turned and reached into a cabinet behind herself, removing a crockery pitcher that she then filled with water. And he kept watching as she silently arranged the carnations one by one inside it.

"Come on," he cajoled in the most gentle voice he could muster. "Make a wish and blow out the candles."

She glanced up from her task of arranging the flowers, stared at him in silence for a moment longer, then shook her head.

"Okay, then," he told her. "*I'll* make a wish and blow out the candles."

He thought for a moment, then realized he knew the perfect thing to wish for for Lucy. He strode over to the table and, bending over, he closed his eyes, made a wish, inhaled a deep breath and expelled it in a quick rush of air. When he opened his eyes again, a white wisp of smoke spiraled up from each candle.

"There you go," he said with a grin, "you're going to get your wish."

"No, *you're* going to get *your* wish," Lucy corrected him.

His grin grew broader. "Then we're both in for a treat, aren't we?"

She eyed him suspiciously. "Depends on what you wished for."

Boone glanced down at the cake, feigning nonchalance as he swiped his finger over the frosting at one end and sucked it into his mouth. "Yeah, I guess it does," he told her after swallowing.

She seemed to take an inordinate amount of interest in his activity, but her expression quickly cleared. "So you going to tell me what you wished for or not?" she asked him.

He moved toward her again, pausing when scarcely a breath of air separated them. Then, flattening one palm on the counter beside her, he leaned forward, the action bringing his face very close to hers. Softly, quietly, he said, "If I tell you what I wished for, it won't come true."

She ducked her head to avoid looking at him, gave a perfunctory spin to a couple of carnations in the pitcher on the counter, then turned to lean against it again. "What difference does it make?'' she asked, her voice a little unsteady. ''It's not going to come true, anyway.''

Boone pressed his other hand against the counter on the other side of her, moving his body directly in front of hers, leaving just enough air between the two of them to provide a little breathing space. Because Lucy's breathing suddenly seemed to be coming in deep, ragged gasps that caused her chest to rise and fall quickly beneath the softly worn flannel of her pajama top and the even-more-softly worn undershirt beneath.

The undershirt was so worn, in fact, that Boone could see the faint outline of the dusky valley between her breasts and knew she wasn't wearing a bra. And inevitably he remembered that her skin there was as soft and creamy as that on her face, her throat, her neck....

''If it doesn't make any difference what I wished for,'' he said quietly, ''then why are you so worried about it?''

''I—I'm not worried.''

''You seem to be worried about something.''

''Well, I'm not.''

But Boone could tell by the way her pulse danced against the soft skin of her throat that she was lying. He leaned forward even more and detected a hint of that clean, soapy fragrance again, and he found it oddly arousing.

''I don't believe you,'' he said softly.

Her eyes widened, though whether in surprise, shock or surrender, he couldn't be sure. ''It doesn't matter what you... what you believe,'' she stammered.

He moved until his body was flush against hers, their hearts pounding erratically almost as one. ''Doesn't it?''

''No.''

For a long moment he only stood before her, gazing down at the worried expression on her face, marveling at the way she seemed to be looking at everything in the room but him. Which was no small feat, seeing as how he was doing his best to block her view of anything but him. To up the stakes he pushed himself closer to her still, until their bodies were touching from shoulder to knee.

He expected Lucy to shove him away, or at least to duck around under his arm and make her escape. Instead when he moved closer to her, when he touched his body to hers, she looked up and met his gaze levelly, eye to eye.

And immediately he felt himself falling. Falling into the dangerous depths of those blue, blue eyes, nearly drowning in the wild eddy of emotions spinning there. Then, thankfully, she dropped her gaze again, and Boone's lungs began functioning once more. Suddenly he felt as if he'd known her forever. And suddenly he felt as if she were the answer to every question he'd ever asked about life. Because even if she hadn't already admitted as much to him, he could see that her feelings for him ran deep and ran strong. Perhaps even as deep and as strong as his feelings were for her.

"Lucy," he said softly.

"What?"

"Look at me."

Slowly, almost shyly, she lifted her head again to meet his gaze. Her eyes were dry, but depthless. In the faint light of a single lamp burning over the stove, her pupils had expanded to nearly the edge of her irises, creating the impression that her eyes were dark, unending vessels of emotion. And without warning, he felt himself falling into that eternity all over again.

Suddenly, without warning, Boone found himself kissing Lucy.

He kissed her with all the need and wanting that had been building inside him for as long as he could remember, covering her mouth with his in an effort to drink his fill of her. And once he tasted her, he knew there would be no turning back. Not that he had ever intended to. Lucy tasted of longing and loneliness. She tasted of solitude and sorrow. Boone recognized her essence immediately because it was so similar to his own. In many ways, he suddenly realized, the two of them were very much alike. And for that, and so many other things, he never wanted to let her go.

Lucy wasn't sure what exactly had happened or why Boone had leaned forward and kissed her so sweetly, so gently. All she knew was that one minute she was trying to think of a way to make him go home and leave her alone to salvage what she could of her dignity, and the next she was clinging to him as if she had no dignity left.

His mouth on hers was warm and willing, beguilingly insistent. For one brief moment she told herself to retreat from his embrace, cautioned herself that if she let things go any further, there would be no turning back. And then she realized she didn't want to turn back. What she did want was to lose herself to Boone's touch until she forgot all the melancholy little things in life that had ever made her feel incomplete.

And then, as quickly as he'd started kissing her, he stopped. He pulled back far enough to gaze into her eyes, as if he were giving her the opportunity to shove him away from her once and for all. He touched her nowhere, but their bodies remained tantalizingly close. Close enough that even that tiny separation suddenly became intolerable to Lucy. So, her eyes never leaving his, she cupped her hand gently over his rough jaw and traced her thumb along the length of the full lower lip that had taunted her for months.

He opened his mouth as if to speak, and his warm breath skittered over the pad of her thumb. Lucy closed her eyes for a moment, long enough to reassure herself that she wasn't dreaming the entire episode. When she opened them again, Boone was still watching her with that heavy-lidded, too-steady gaze that made her heart race wildly.

He moved his hand to the back of her head, stroking her hair with his open palm, caressing her scalp with strong fingers. The gesture was gentle, rhythmic, hypnotic, intoxicating. And she wanted more than anything for him to repeat the action on other parts of her body that grew more and more jealous with each brush of his fingertips.

She tried to say his name, tried to do something that would put an end to the odd heat that had arisen between them before it burned them both to the core. But for some reason, any protest she might have uttered remained firmly caught in her throat. Instead she leaned back into his caress, tilting her head first one way and then the other, in much the way Mack accommodated his own body to her petting. Boone dipped his hand lower then, curling his fingers warmly around her nape. He pulled her forward again and bent his head to hers once more.

This time when his mouth joined with hers, it was with a gentle exploration and tentative touch. He brushed his lips over hers once, twice, three times, then nuzzled her cheek against his. His jaw was hot and rough, so utterly different from her own, yet so perfectly complementary.

Helplessly she splayed her hands open over his chest, clutching his shirt in her fists as she pulled him closer, inhaling great gulps of his scent as he drew nearer. She ducked her head into the hollow of his neck and kissed him there, dragging her lips along the strong column of his throat and the lean curve of his jaw, a turbulent tremor shaking her as she tasted the salty, masculine flavor of him.

She buried her hands in his hair, tangling the restive tresses in her fingers, tightening her hold when he started to move away from her again. Urging his head back down to hers, Lucy kissed his mouth again fiercely, with all the need and passion she had been forced to keep locked away in a dark, lonely place deep inside her for too long.

Suddenly she knew exactly what she would wish for if given the opportunity to wish again. If she could light her birthday candles one more time and whisper a wish with the breath that extinguished them, she would wish for Boone to make her feel this way forever.

But that would never happen, she reminded herself. She wasn't the woman for him.

Slowly, reluctantly, she ended the kiss to gaze upon his face. His expression was at once puzzled, anxious and eager.

"Why are you doing this?" she asked him softly. "Because I still owe you a day?"

He smiled and shook his head. "No. Because *I* owe *you* a lifetime."

She narrowed her eyes in confusion, then opened her mouth to object. But something in his expression silenced her. "Why would you owe me anything?" she asked him instead.

He curled a finger against her chin and brushed it slowly along the length of her jaw, then curved his palm around her nape and lowered his forehead to hers. "Because I have to make it up to you for ever doubting your word."

She shook her head slowly, still confused. "I don't understand."

"You made a promise to me, Lucy," he reminded her. "And you kept your word. You can't possibly understand how much that meant to me. And I don't know how I ever could have doubted you. For that, I owe you my apologies. And so much more."

"But I haven't kept my promise," she pointed out. "I still owe you one day."

He brought his head back to gaze down into her eyes. "Or one night," he corrected her with a warm grin.

She shook her head again, more resolutely this time. "No, Boone. I won't pay you back like that. It wouldn't be right."

He paused only a heartbeat before asking, "Not even if you were my wife?"

"No, not even I was your—" She stopped abruptly before uttering the final word, her gaze locked with his. "What did you say?"

His smile grew broader. "I'm pretty sure I just asked you to marry me."

"But...why?"

"Um, wait a minute...let me think..." He rolled his eyes toward the ceiling and feigned thought. "Could it be because...I *owe* you? No, wait—that's not it. Hmm...give me another minute...." He thought for a moment more. "Because I *want* you? Yeah, that's part of it...." He returned his gaze to hers, his eyes lit with a merry fire. "But I think mainly it's because I love you."

"But you can't," she said, wondering why she was objecting to the words she'd always wanted to hear.

Boone chuckled. "I can't? Why not?"

"Because you told me you'd never love anyone again, not in this lifetime."

He seemed genuinely baffled by her reminder. "When did I say something stupid like that?"

"After I found that picture of you and your fiancée, you said—"

"Ex-fiancée," he said, correcting her. Again.

"Whatever. You said you'd never—"

He suddenly seemed to remember, because his features cleared. "No, no, no, that's not what I was talking about. What I meant when I said that was—" He seemed to be growing impatient. "Look, I'll explain it to you some other time. Right now, I need to know if you're going to pay me that day you still owe me. Then I can pay you back for doubting your word."

Warming to his playfulness, now that she realized things were looking up, Lucy smiled back and said, "You know, that *is* a pretty big debt. Just how are you planning to pay me back, anyway?"

He pulled her close again, seeming relieved by her question. "I was thinking maybe I could be your slave for a while. Say about five decades or so."

The weight that had settled over her heart began to melt away. "Oh, now *that* sounds like the kind of marriage that could work," she told him.

"So you'll marry me?"

He wasn't nearly as complacent about asking the question as he seemed, she noted. So, just to make him squirm, she chewed her lip anxiously for a moment, pretending she couldn't quite decide. "Do you love me, Boone? Really?"

He bent to kiss her again, a caress of his lips that was full of warmth and wonder, passion and promise. And without him having to say a word, she knew he was speaking the truth.

"I love you more than you'll ever know," he murmured.

She smiled. "I think I know."

"Now about that marriage business…?"

She nodded. "I think it's the least you can do, seeing as how much you owe me for ever doubting my word."

He dipped his head to her shoulder and began to lightly nibble on her neck. "Did I mention that you'd be my slave every other weekend?"

She shook her head. "No. You sorta missed that part."

"Well, I still own you for one day. My wish is your command, right? For another twenty-four hours?"

The warm flicker of his tongue against her earlobe made her sigh, and she knew that she would agree to whatever he wished. "Oh, yeah…" she purred.

"Then first, I'm commanding you to marry me. And next, I'm commanding that we each get one night a week to be…you know…enslaved."

Lucy thought that sounded like a very good idea indeed. "Okay."

"Okay what?" he asked. "Okay you'll marry me? Okay you'll enslave me? Okay you'll let me do all those things I did to you before, when it's my turn?"

But Lucy only smiled and said, "Okay."

"That's all I need to hear. So, Lucy," he added, pulling her collar away from her throat to string a series of light kisses along her shoulder.

"Hmm?" she asked, a ripple of delight eddying everywhere he touched his mouth to her skin.

"Have you bought any…bedroom furniture yet?"

"Oh, Boone… O-only a mattress and box springs," she whispered when she felt the tip of his tongue skim down along her collarbone. "I, uh, haven't been able to decide on anything for that room, either."

"Well, at least you've got the main thing."

"Mmm…"

"So where is it?"

"Hmm?"

"Your bedroom, Lucy. Where is it?"

"Mmm...oh, that." She waved her hand negligibly over his shoulder, in the general vicinity of the doorway. "Oh, it's...up there...somewhere...you can't miss it."

He paused in nibbling the delicate skin just above her breast, and when Lucy opened her eyes, she saw that he was looking over his shoulder, his gaze following the direction her hand had indicated. But when she, too, glanced over his shoulder to see what precisely he was looking at, she realized it wasn't the door. Instead he seemed to be contemplating...the kitchen table?

"Then again," he said, "beds can be highly overrated."

She turned to meet his gaze. "You can't be serious."

"Oh, can't I?"

"No, Boone, we can't."

"Oh, can't we?"

"No!" she exclaimed, laughing.

"Lucy, Lucy, Lucy," he said with a slow shake of his head. "Need I remind you yet again that you're my slave?"

"Oh?" she asked haughtily. "And when do I get my turn to tell you what to do?"

He smiled. "I was under the impression that you'd be taking over the minute the minister says, 'I now pronounce you husband and wife.'"

She arched her brows in thought. "We could write our own ceremony," she suggested. "And just have him say, 'I now pronounce you slave and master.'"

Boone pushed her pajama shirt from her shoulders, letting it fall to the floor in a pool of soft flannel. Then he hooked a finger beneath one strap of her undershirt and skimmed that off her shoulder, too. "I have a better one," he said as he rubbed his lips gently over the skin he exposed. "How about, 'Gentlemen, start your engines'?"

Lucy's engine was already rumbling nicely, thanks to Boone. And since he didn't seem to require a reply, so intent was he on the expanse of shoulder he'd revealed by shedding her shirt, she didn't offer one. Instead, she leaned forward to touch her mouth to his neck, brushing her lips lightly over the rough, warm skin she encountered.

She felt his hands at her waist lifting her, and instinctively, she looped her arms around his neck and grazed his cheek with hers, loving the scratchy feel of his day-old beard as it abraded her jaw. The next thing she knew, she was seated on the edge of her kitchen table, and Boone had insinuated himself between her legs.

"You're really serious about this, aren't you?" she whispered against his ear.

In response, he dipped his fingers below the hem of her undershirt and began to push the soft fabric upward, until he had it bunched beneath her arms with her breasts fully exposed. Without further hesitation, he leaned toward her, sucking her nipple full into his mouth and laving it with the flat of his tongue. Lucy wound her fingers tightly in his hair and pulled him close, her head falling back, her eyes fluttering closed.

For long moments he held her there, his hands firm on her waist, his mouth insistent at her breast. Then Lucy felt his thumbs pressing into her ribs, his hands palming all the way up her torso until he curved both below her breasts. He closed his hands over each completely and cupped her with sure fingers, lightly squeezing her warm flesh as he suckled first one breast, then the other, so sweetly, so fiercely that she thought she would burst with wanting him.

The fingers she tangled in his hair flexed more resolutely, a silent indication that she wanted more. So Boone dropped one hand to the waistband of her pajama bottoms and deftly dipped his fingers inside. When she opened her legs wider to accommodate his touch, he found her naked beneath the fabric, her swollen womanhood warm and waiting for him. He brushed his fingers lightly over her, until she removed a hand from his hair to place it over her pajamas, guiding his marauding fingers more intimately against herself.

She helped him stroke her over and over, urging him deeper and deeper, harder and harder, faster and faster, until together, they brought her to ecstasy. Then Lucy pushed her whole body closer to Boone with a more insistent demand. Instead of removing his hand from her pajamas, he simply skimmed it around until he cupped her warm bottom in his palm. Then, with his other hand, he pushed the soft fabric away, tugging Lucy's hips forward until they tipped backward and she was fully open to him.

Then he stepped back long enough to unfasten his belt and jerk open the buttons of his fly. Lucy watched, heavy-lidded, lips half-parted, as he freed himself from his jeans, then she reached out to wrap a fist in his shirt and yanked him toward herself again. Boone circled her calves with firm fingers, and roped her legs around his waist, hooking her ankles at the small of his back. With her undershirt still bunched above her breasts, she fell back on the table, propping herself on her elbows so she could see his face as he entered her.

He did so with a single swift, solid thrust, and they both cried out at the full feeling of completion. Slowly, so that she could feel the friction of every inch of him sliding against her, Boone withdrew, only to grip her hips more fiercely so that he could pummel her again. This time when he ground himself into her, Lucy's head fell backward, and her whole body seemed to shudder at his advance. Boone paused for a moment, fearful that he had hurt her somehow.

Then she rolled her head forward again, met his gaze levelly and whispered, "More. I want more."

Whatever she wanted, he thought. He was, after all, her slave, and had been virtually since the moment they'd met.

He pulled himself from her once more, shifted her position on the table so that he could invade her more deeply, then bolted inside her again. A spasm of delight caught him, and for a moment, Boone could only stand still and revel in being so close to her again. Then he began to move himself in and out of her, his rhythm building slowly, until all he could feel was Lucy. Deeper and deeper he drove himself, deeper and deeper he fell, until he was as much a part of her as she had become of him.

And when it seemed he would never be closer to perfection than he was at that moment, Lucy took him further still, shoving her hips toward him, pulling him deeper inside her than he'd ever been before. He was hers. Plain and simple. And she would always be his.

His completion this time was even more explosive than the first had been, and he shuddered violently as he emptied himself inside her. Lucy cried his name over and over and over, her voice joining his as he likewise beckoned to her. He pulled her forward and into his arms, and she squeezed her legs more fiercely around his waist. He held her that way as he carried her through the house, astounded he had the strength to do so, until he found her bedroom and fell alongside her on the bed.

Their hearts beat rapid-fire against each other as they lay side by side, and all Lucy could do was gaze in wonder at the man who had saved her life. Not because he'd carried her from a burning building, but because he had given her the love she had wanted and needed for so long, a love to rival the one she felt for him.

"I love you, Boone," she whispered in the darkness.

"I love you, Lucy," he immediately replied.

They lay in comfortable, complete contentment for a moment, then Lucy remembered that today was her birthday. "By the way," she asked, feeling lethargy creep up to claim her entire body. "What did you wish for when you blew out the candles?"

She felt the sigh well up inside him before it even passed through his lips. "I wished that you would find your family," he said softly.

She snuggled closer and tucked her head into the hollow of his throat. "Wow. That must be a speed record for wishes coming true."

She felt him smile as he tilted his head to kiss her cheek. And then, for the first time in a long time, Lucy fell asleep in no way worried about what tomorrow would bring.

Epilogue

"Lucy! He did it again!"

Boone stood on the front porch and curled his lip in disgust at the dead...thing...lying on the steps in front of the mailbox. He didn't want to get close enough to see what exactly it was. But he knew without question how it had come to be lying there.

Ever since he had married Lucy nearly a year ago and moved himself and his furniture into her house—*their* house, he corrected himself automatically, and *their* furniture—Mack had taken great delight in dropping some poor dead creature at Boone's feet at least once a week. Lucy had assured him on countless occasions that it was Mack's way of making up for all the hard times he'd given Boone in the past. Boone, however, was convinced that each and every offering was a not-so-subtle threat.

"Lucy!" he called out again.

She appeared in the doorway behind him with a broom and dustpan and shooed him out of the way. Boone tried not to gag as she swept up whatever it was and deposited it into a paper bag. She turned to look at him, but her expression wasn't exactly reassuring.

"I'll talk to him," she said. "But I can't make any promises. He only does it because he likes you. And, truth be told, I think he's trying to impress you. It's that whole father-son competition thing."

Boone gritted his teeth at her. "I am *not* his father."

"Well, you know what I mean. He does these things because he cares about you."

"Oh, yeah, like all those attempts to flay my flesh that you call love nips, right?"

"Well, that's what they are."

"Lucy, he's drawn blood at least twice."

"Well, that just means that he *really* likes you."

"Oh, I doubt that."

Boone reached into the mailbox and withdrew the usual— the water bill, the electric bill, the phone bill…assorted advertisements for an upcoming President's Day sale… something telling him he may already be a winner—but then, he already knew that, he thought, gazing over at his wife. And then, under everything else, something interesting.

"Did you hire another private investigator to find your brother?" he asked Lucy, fingering a thin white envelope curiously.

She shook her head. "No, why?"

"Here's something from a Roxanne Matheny, P.I., addressed to you," he said, handing the letter over to Lucy.

She scanned the return address. "Washington, D.C.," she muttered. "I've never heard of her."

"Well, she's obviously heard of you."

Lucy ran her thumb under the flap of the envelope, then withdrew a typed letter and shook it open. As Boone watched, her face went white, and before he realized what was happening, her legs buckled beneath her, and she fell hard on her bottom to the porch step below.

"Lucy?" he asked, alarmed. He quickly sat beside her and curled an arm around her waist. "What is it?"

She covered her mouth with one hand as she read, the other hand trembling as her fingers tightened on the letter. Her eyes filled with tears so quickly they spilled down her cheeks unchecked. "Oh, God," she said. But instead of elaborating, she began to read the letter again.

"What is it?" Boone repeated, pulling her close, trying in vain to read the letter over her shoulder. "What's wrong?"

"Nothing," she whispered roughly. "Nothing's wrong. Everything's...oh, Boone."

She threw her arms around his neck and climbed into his lap, crowding herself close. Sobs wracked her body for several moments, and all he could do was hold her and rub her back and murmur soothing words. Finally, when her crying subsided some, he pulled her gently away.

"What is it, Lucy?"

She just shook her head silently and held up the letter for him to see. As Boone scanned the missive, Lucy wiped her eyes dry and swiped a finger under her nose.

"She's writing on behalf of my brother," she finally said. "He's been looking for me for more than a year now. He's been in D.C. all this time. Boone, he's practically been my next-door neighbor and I didn't even know it."

Boone turned his gaze to his wife's and smiled. "Small world," he said with a soft chuckle.

"He wants to meet me," Lucy said. "He wants...he wants me, Boone. He...he wants me."

She began to cry freely again, turning her face to his chest for support. Boone stroked a hand over her back and kissed her hair and marveled again that she could ever have doubted it.

"Of course he wants you, Lucy," Boone said quietly. "And now you'll have that family you've always wanted."

She pushed herself away from him and cupped his jaw in her palm. "Oh, Boone," she said with a shaky sigh. "I've already got my family. Right here. With you and Mack."

He tightened his arms around her, but said nothing, letting the warmth her words brought with them filter through every cell in his body.

"But this," she added, lifting the letter again, "this is like an added bonus. Like a surprise little blessing. It's..."

She swiped at her eyes again and smiled. Then she seemed to suddenly remember something, because she turned to Boone with a look that was almost panicked. "I wonder if this means she found my other brother, too."

Boone's eyebrows shot up in surprise. "Your *other* brother? What other brother? What are you talking about?"

She narrowed her eyes at him, obviously as confused as he was. "Didn't I mention that in addition to my twin brother I also have an older brother?"

Boone gaped at her. "No, you never mentioned that."

"Are you sure?" she asked. "I mean, that's kind of important, Boone."

"I *know* it's important, Lucy...." He shook his head at her in wonder, asking himself why he was so surprised by this new development. "So you have a big brother, too?"

She nodded and sniffled again. "I'm pretty sure. Not as certain as I am about my twin, but I do remember there being three of us. At least, I think there were." She glanced down at the letter again. "If this Roxanne Matheny found me, surely she could find another brother, right? I mean, assuming he exists. Which he does. I think."

"So are you going to contact her?" Boone asked, knowing the answer to the question already.

She nodded. "Yeah. I am. I need to tell my twin brother something."

"What's that?"

"That he's going to be an uncle."

Boone nodded. "He'll be glad to hear th—" He snapped his head around again when he realized exactly what she had said. "He's going to be a what?"

She smiled and wound an errant curl around her fingertip. "An uncle," she repeated.

"Which would mean you're going to be a—"

"Mother," Lucy confirmed with a nod.

"And I'm going to be a—"

"Father. Yep, that you are."

He let that sink in for a moment, then after a minute he yanked her into his arms. "Oh, boy," he mumbled into her hair.

"Or maybe a girl," she said with a laugh. "We won't know for a few months."

"It doesn't matter," he told her. "All that matters is that *this* kid won't ever have to worry about parents who go back on their word, or who don't appreciate a child for what that child is."

"And just what is a child?" she asked, hugging him back.

"It's a promise, Lucy. That's what it is. A promise of nothing but good things to come."

They held each other for a long time on the front stoop, unheedful of the cold winter wind that ruffled their hair and blushed their faces, each planning their family in ways they'd never considered before. And each decided quickly that it was something they should have done a long, long time ago.

* * * * *

Beginning next month from

▼ SILHOUETTE®
Desire

by
**Elizabeth
Bevarly**

Watch as three siblings separated in childhood
are reunited and find love along the way!

ROXY AND THE RICH MAN (D #1053, February 1997)—
Wealthy businessman Spencer Melbourne finds love with the
sexy female detective he hires to find his long-lost twin.

LUCY AND THE LONER (D #1063, April 1997)—
Independent Lucy Dolan shows her gratitude to the fire
fighter who comes to her rescue—by becoming his slave
for a month.

And coming your way in July 1997—
THE FAMILY McCORMICK continues with the wonderful
story of the oldest McCormick sibling. Don't miss any of
these delightful stories. Only from Silhouette Desire.

Take 4 bestselling love stories FREE

Plus get a FREE surprise gift!

Special Limited-time Offer

Mail to Silhouette Reader Service™

P.O. Box 609
Fort Erie, Ontario
L2A 5X3

YES! Please send me 4 free Silhouette Desire® novels and my free surprise gift. Then send me 6 brand-new novels every month, which I will receive months before they appear in bookstores. Bill me at the low price of $3.24 each plus 25¢ delivery and GST*. That's the complete price and a savings of over 10% off the cover prices—quite a bargain! I understand that accepting the books and gift places me under no obligation ever to buy any books. I can always return a shipment and cancel at any time. Even if I never buy another book from Silhouette, the 4 free books and the surprise gift are mine to keep forever.

326 BPA A3UY

Name	(PLEASE PRINT)	
Address	Apt. No.	
City	Province	Postal Code

This offer is limited to one order per household and not valid to present Silhouette Desire® subscribers. *Terms and prices are subject to change without notice. Canadian residents will be charged applicable provincial taxes and GST.

CDES-696 ©1990 Harlequin Enterprises Limited

As seen on TV!
Free Gift Offer

With a Free Gift proof-of-purchase from any Silhouette® book,
you can receive a beautiful cubic zirconia pendant.

This gorgeous marquise-shaped stone is a genuine cubic
zirconia—accented by an 18" gold tone necklace.

(Approximate retail value $19.95)

Send for yours today...
compliments of ▼ *Silhouette*®
TM

To receive your free gift, a cubic zirconia pendant, send us one original proof-of-
purchase, photocopies not accepted, from the back of any Silhouette Romance™,
Silhouette Desire®, Silhouette Special Edition®, Silhouette Intimate Moments®
or Silhouette Yours Truly™ title available in February, March and April at your favorite
retail outlet, together with the Free Gift Certificate, plus a check or money order for
$1.65 u.s./$2.15 can. (do not send cash) to cover postage and handling, payable
to Silhouette Free Gift Offer. We will send you the specified gift. Allow 6 to 8 weeks for
delivery. Offer good until April 30, 1997 or while quantities last. Offer valid in the
U.S. and Canada only.

Free Gift Certificate

Name: _____

Address: _____

City: _____ State/Province: _____ Zip/Postal Code: _____

Mail this certificate, one proof-of-purchase and a check or money order for postage
and handling to: SILHOUETTE FREE GIFT OFFER 1997. In the U.S.: 3010 Walden
Avenue, P.O. Box 9077, Buffalo NY 14269-9077. In Canada: P.O. Box 613, Fort Erie,
Ontario L2Z 5X3.

FREE GIFT OFFER   084-KFD
ONE PROOF-OF-PURCHASE
To collect your fabulous FREE GIFT, a cubic zirconia pendant, you must include this
original proof-of-purchase for each gift with the properly completed Free Gift Certificate.

084-KFD

National Bestselling Author

MARY LYNN BAXTER

"Ms. Baxter's writing…strikes every chord within the
female spirit."
—Sandra Brown

LONE STAR
Heat

SHE is Juliana Reed, a prominent broadcast journalist whose
television show is about to be syndicated. Until the murder…

HE is Gates O'Brien, a high-ranking member of the
Texas Rangers, determined to forget about his ex-wife. He's
onto something bad….

Juliana and Gates are ex-spouses, unwillingly involved in an
explosive circle of political corruption, blackmail and murder.

In order to survive, they must overcome the pain of the past…and
the very demons that drove them apart.

Available in September 1997 at your favorite retail outlet.

IN CELEBRATION OF MOTHER'S DAY, JOIN
SILHOUETTE THIS MAY AS WE BRING YOU

a funny thing
HAPPENED ON THE WAY TO THE
DELIVERY ROOM

THESE THREE STORIES, CELEBRATING THE
LIGHTER SIDE OF MOTHERHOOD, ARE
WRITTEN BY YOUR FAVORITE AUTHORS:

KASEY MICHAELS
KATHLEEN EAGLE
EMILIE RICHARDS

When three couples make the trip to the delivery room, they get more than their own bundles of joy...they get the promise of love!

Available this May,
wherever Silhouette books are sold.